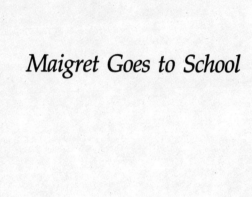

Maigret Goes to School

Georges Simenon

Maigret Goes to School

Translated from the French by Daphne Woodward

A Harvest / HBJ Book
A Helen and Kurt Wolff Book
Harcourt Brace Jovanovich, Publishers
San Diego   New York   London

Requests for permission to make copies
of any part of the work should be mailed to:
Permissions Department,
Harcourt Brace Jovanovich, Publishers, 8th Floor,
Orlando, Florida 32887.

Library of Congress Cataloging-in-Publication Data
Simenon, Georges, 1903–1989
[Maigret à l'école. English]
Maigret goes to school/by Georges Simenon;
translated by Daphne Woodward.
p. cm.
Translation of: Maigret à l'école.
"A Harvest/HBJ book."
"A Helen and Kurt Wolff book."
ISBN 0-15-655156-X (pbk.)
I. Title.
PQ2637.I53M25313 1988
843'.912—dc19 88-971

Printed in the United States of America

First Harvest/HBJ edition 1988

B C D E F G H I J

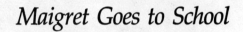

Maigret Goes to School

1

THERE are certain images which one registers unconsciously, with the precision of a camera, and later, recalling them to memory, racks one's brain to discover where this took place.

Maigret had ceased to realize, after so many years, that each time he arrived, always slightly out of breath, at the top of the steep, dusty staircase at Police Headquarters, he would make a brief pause and glance automatically towards the glass cage which served as a waiting-room and was known to some of his colleagues as 'the aquarium', to others as 'Purgatory'. Perhaps they all did this and it had become a kind of professional reflex.

Even on mornings like this, when bright, pale sunlight, gay as lilies-of-the-valley, was shimmering down on Paris and casting a glow on the pink chimney-pots above the roofs, a lamp was kept burning all day in 'Purgatory', which had no window and whose only light came from the immense corridor.

Sometimes one saw, seated in the arm-chairs or on the green velvet chairs, various seedy-looking characters, old-timers picked up by some inspector during the night and now waiting to be questioned, or else stool-pigeons, or witnesses who had received their summons the day before and now raised melancholy heads whenever anyone went by.

For some mysterious reason, this had been chosen as the place to hang the two black frames, with their gold fillets, which held the photographs of policemen killed while on duty.

There were other people who passed through Purgatory, men and women belonging to what is called 'good society'; and they would remain standing at first, as though about to be sent for at any moment—as though they were just here for an unimportant visit. After a longish time they would be seen to move over to a chair on which they would finally sit down, and it was not unusual to find them still there three hours later, shrunk into themselves, mournful-eyed, having lost all sense of their social precedence.

On this particular morning there was only one man in Purgatory, and Maigret noticed that he belonged to the type commonly known as 'rat-faced'. He was on the thin side. His bare, receding forehead was crowned by a fluff of reddish hair. His eyes were doubtless blue or violet, and the forward thrust of his nose was all the more apparent in contrast to his receding chin.

Everywhere, from schooldays onward, we meet people of this kind, and there is, heaven knows why, a tendency not to take them seriously.

Maigret felt he paid so little attention to the man that if, as he opened the door of his own office, he had been asked who was in the waiting-room, he might have been unable to reply. It was five minutes to nine. The window was wide open and a light, goldish-blue haze was drifting up from the Seine. For the first time this year he had put on his thinner overcoat, but the air was still cool; you wanted to drink it in like some light, white wine, and it made the skin on your face feel taut.

Taking off his hat, he glanced at the visiting-card which lay in full view on his blotter. It bore, in pale ink, the words *'Joseph Gastin, schoolmaster'*. And in the right-hand corner, in small letters which he had to bend forward to read, *'Saint-André-sur-Mer'*.

He did not connect this card with the rat-faced man, only wondered where he had heard of Saint-André-sur-Mer. The bell rang in the corridor as a summons to the daily report. He removed his overcoat, picked up the file he had prepared the day before, and set off, as he had done for so many years, to the Chief's office. On the way he met other chief-inspectors, and their eyes all reflected the mood he had noticed in the passers-by in the street.

'This time it's really spring!'

'Seems like it.'

'Going to be a wonderful day.'

Sunshine was pouring in through the big windows of the Chief's office, as though through the windows of a country church, and pigeons were cooing on the stone ledge outside.

Each man, as he came in, rubbed his hands and made the same remark:

'This is spring.'

They were all over forty-five years old; the matters they were about to discuss were serious, in some cases ghastly, but all the same they were as happy as children because of the sudden mildness of the air, and above all because of the light that was flooding down on the city and transforming every street-corner, the house-fronts, the roofs, the cars crossing the Pont Saint-Michel, into pictures that one would have liked to hang on the wall.

'Have you seen the assistant manager of the bank in the Rue de Rivoli, Maigret?'

'I have an appointment with him in half an hour.'

An unimportant affair. This was an almost empty week. The assistant manager of the branch office of a bank in the Rue de Rivoli, just near the central markets, suspected one of his clerks of dishonesty.

He filled his pipe and looked out of a window while his colleague from General Information was discussing another matter—some business about a Senator's daughter who had got herself into an awkward situation.

Back in his own office, he found Lucas waiting, with his hat already on, to go to the Rue de Rivoli with him.

'Shall we walk?'

It was quite near. Maigret didn't give another thought to the visiting-card. Going past Purgatory, he saw the rat-faced man again, and two or three other 'clients', one of whom was a nightclub proprietor whom he recognized and who was there because of the Senator's daughter.

They walked to the Pont Neuf, the pair of them, Maigret with long strides, and the short-legged Lucas obliged to take many more steps in order to keep up with him. They couldn't have said, afterwards, what they had talked about. Perhaps they had merely been looking around them. In the Rue de Rivoli there was a strong smell of vegetables and fruit, and lorries were removing loads of crates and baskets.

They went into the bank, listened to the assistant manager's explanations, walked round the premises, casting sidelong glances at the suspected clerk.

For lack of proofs, they decided to set a trap for him. They discussed the details, then said good-bye. Maigret and Lucas left and found it so warm outside that they carried their overcoats instead of putting them on again, which gave them a kind of holiday feeling.

In the Place Dauphine, they stopped with one accord.

'Shall we have a quick one?'

It was too early for an *apéritif*, but they both

felt that the taste of *pernod* would make a wonderful accompaniment to the spring atmosphere, and in they went to the Brasserie Dauphine.

'Two *pernods*, quickly!'

'D'you happen to know Saint-André-sur-Mer?'

'Isn't it somewhere in the Charentes?'

This reminded Maigret of the beach at Fourras, in the sunshine, the oysters he had eaten at about this time, half past ten in the morning, on the terrace of a little *bistrot*, washing them down with a bottle of the local white wine, at the bottom of which lay a few grains of sand.

'Think that clerk is a swindler?'

'His boss seems positive about it.'

'He looked a poor devil to me.'

'We shall know in a couple of days.'

They strolled along the Quai des Orfèvres, went up the big staircase, and once again Maigret paused. Rat-face was still there, leaning forward, his long, bony hands clasped on his knees. He looked up at Maigret with what the chief-inspector felt to be a reproachful expression.

In his office he found the visiting-card lying where he had left it, and rang for the office-boy.

'Is he still here?'

'Ever since eight o'clock. He was here before me. He insists on speaking to you personally.'

Any number of people, most of them mad or half-crazy, used to ask to speak personally to the Chief or to Maigret, whose names they had come to know from the newspapers. They would refuse to be fobbed off with an inspector, and some would wait all day and come back next morning, standing up hopefully whenever the chief-inspector went by, only to sit down and wait again.

'Bring him in.'

He sat down, filled two or three pipes, signed to the man, when he was shown in, to sit down opposite him. Picking up the visiting-card, he asked:

'Is this yours?'

Looking more closely, he realized that the man had probably had no sleep, for he was grey-faced, with red eyelids and unnaturally bright eyes. His hands were folded, as they had been in the waiting-room, with the fingers clenched so tightly that the joints cracked.

Instead of answering the question, he muttered, with an anxious yet resigned glance at the chief-inspector:

'You know about it?'

'About what?'

The man looked surprised, confused, disappointed perhaps.

'I thought it was already known. I left Saint-André yesterday evening and a journalist had arrived by then. I took the night train. I've come straight here.'

'Why?'

He seemed to be intelligent, but was obviously very upset and didn't know where to begin his story. Maigret awed him. He had doubtless known him by repute for a long time and, like a lot of people, looked upon him as someone endowed with almost divine powers.

At a distance he had thought it would be easy. But now he was confronted by a man in flesh and blood, smoking his pipe with short puffs and watching him with wide-open, almost expressionless eyes.

Was that how he had imagined him? Wasn't he beginning to be sorry he had come?

'They must be thinking I've run away,' he said nervously, with a bitter smile. 'If I were guilty, as they feel sure I am, and if I'd meant to run away, I shouldn't be here now, should I?'

'I can't very well answer that question till I know more about it,' murmured Maigret. 'What are you accused of?'

'Of killing Léonie Birard.'

'Who's accusing you?'

'The whole village, more or less openly. The local police chief didn't dare to arrest me. He admitted frankly that he hadn't sufficient evidence, but he asked me not to go away.'

'All the same, you went?'

'Yes.'

'Why?'

The visitor, too tense to remain seated for long, sprang to his feet, stuttering:

'Do you mind?'

He didn't know where to stand or what to do with himself.

'I sometimes even forget what's going on.'

He pulled a grubby handkerchief from his

pocket, mopped his forehead. The handkerchief probably still smelt of the train, and of his sweat.

'Have you had breakfast?'

'No. I was in a hurry to get here. Above all, I didn't want to be arrested before that, you understand.'

How could Maigret have understood?

'Why, exactly, have you come to see me?'

'Because I have confidence in you. I know that if you will, you can find out the truth.'

'When did this lady . . . what did you say her name was?'

'Léonie Birard. She used to be our postmistress.'

'When did she die?'

'She was killed on Tuesday morning. The day before yesterday. Soon after ten o'clock in the morning.'

'And you are being accused of the crime?'

'You were born in the country, I saw that in a magazine. You spent most of your childhood there. So you must know the sort of thing that happens in a small village. The population of Saint-André is only three hundred and twenty.'

'Just a minute. This crime was committed in the Charentes?'

'Yes. About nine miles north-west of La Rochelle, not far from the Aiguillon headland. You know it?'

'A little. But it so happens that I belong to Police Headquarters in Paris and have no authority in the Charentes.'

'I thought of that.'

'Well, then . . .'

The man was wearing his best suit, which was threadbare; his shirt had a frayed collar. Standing in the middle of the room he had his head lowered, and was staring at the carpet.

'Of course . . .' he sighed.

'What do you mean?'

'I was wrong. I don't know, now. It seemed quite natural at the time.'

'What did?'

'Coming to put myself under your protection.'

'Under my protection?' repeated Maigret in surprise.

Gastin ventured to glance at him, with the air of a man wondering how he stands.

'Down there, even if they don't arrest me, something unpleasant may happen to me.'

'They don't like you?'

'No.'

'Why not?'

'In the first place, because I'm the schoolmaster and the secretary of the *mairie*.'

'I don't understand.'

'It's a long time since you lived in the country. They've all got money. They're farmers or else *bouchoteurs*. You know the *bouchots*?'

'The mussel-beds, along the coast?'

'Yes. We're right in the *bouchot* and oyster district. Everybody owns at least part of one. It's very profitable. They're rich. Nearly everyone has a car or a small van. But do you know how many of them pay income-tax?'

'Very few, I dare say.'

'Not one! In our village, the doctor and I are the only tax-payers. Naturally, they call me an idler. They imagine it's they who pay my salary. When I complain because the children don't come to school, they tell me to mind my own business. And when I told my pupils to touch their caps to me in the street, they asked me who I thought I was.'

'Tell me about the Léonie Birard business.'

'You mean it?'

With the return of hope, his expression had become firmer. He made himself sit down, tried to speak calmly, though he could not prevent his voice from trembling with ill-controlled emotion.

'You'd need to know the lay-out of the village. It's difficult to explain at this distance. As in almost all villages, the school is just behind the *mairie*. I live there too, on the other side of the courtyard, and I have a scrap of kitchen-garden. On Tuesday, the day before yesterday, the weather was just about what it is today, a real spring day, and it was a neap-tide.'

'Is that important?'

'At the neap-tide, that is to say during the period when the ebb and flow of the tides is slight, nobody goes out for mussels or oysters. You understand?'

'Yes.'

'Beyond the school playground there are gardens and the backs of several houses, including Léonie Birard's.'

'What sort of age was she?'

11

'Sixty-six. Being the secretary of the *mairie*, I know everyone's exact age.'

'Of course.'

'She retired eight years ago and became practically crippled. She never goes out any more, and hobbles round the house with a stick. She's a nasty woman.'

'In what way nasty?'

'She hates everybody.'

'Why?'

'I don't know. She's never married. She had a niece who lived with her a long time and who's married to Julien, the ironmonger, who is also the village policeman.'

On another day Maigret might have found these stories boring. That morning, what with the sun shining in through his window and bringing a spring-like warmth with it, and his pipe which had an unaccustomed taste, he was listening with a vague smile to words that reminded him of another village, which had also had its dramatic incidents between the postmistress, the schoolmaster and the village policeman.

'The two women aren't on speaking terms any longer, because Léonie didn't want her niece to get married. She's not on speaking terms with Dr. Bresselles, either; she said he'd tried to poison her with his drugs.'

'Did he try to poison her?'

'Of course not! That's just to show you the kind of woman she is, or rather was. When she was postmistress she used to listen in on telephone calls, read postcards, so that she knew everyone's secrets. She found no difficulty in working up bad feeling between people. Most quarrels in families or between neighbours were started by her.'

'So she wasn't popular?'

'She certainly wasn't.'

'Well, then . . .'

Maigret's manner suggested that this simplified everything, that the death of a woman who was universally hated could bring nothing but delight to everyone.

'But I'm not popular either.'

'Because of what you told me?'

'Because of that and all the rest. I'm not a local man. I was born in Paris, in the Rue Caulaincourt in the XVIIIth *arrondissement*, and my wife comes from the Rue Lamarck.'

'Does your wife live at Saint-André with you?'

'We live together, with our son, who's thirteen years old.'

'Does he go to your school?'

'There's no other for him to go to.'

'Do the other boys hold it against him, that he's the teacher's son?'

Maigret remembered about that, too. He remembered it from his own boyhood. The tenant-farmers' sons had held it against him that his father was the estate manager, to whom their fathers had to submit accounts.

'I don't favour him, I assure you. In fact I rather suspect he purposely works less well than he could.'

13

He had gradually calmed down. His eyes had lost their frightened expression. This was no lunatic, inventing a story to make himself interesting.

'Léonie Birard had developed a special dislike of me.'

'For no reason?'

'She used to say I stirred up the children against her. But that was quite untrue, Inspector. On the contrary, I always tried to make them behave politely. She was very fat, huge in fact. It seems she wore a wig. And she had a hairy face, a definite moustache and black bristles on her chin. That's enough to set the children off, don't you see? Added to which, she would get into a rage at the slightest thing, for instance, if she saw some child peering in at her window and putting its tongue out. She'd get up from her arm-chair and shake her stick threateningly. That amused them. One of their favourite games was to go and make old mother Birard angry.'

Hadn't there been an old woman like that in his own village? In his day it was old mother Tatin, who kept the draper's shop, and the children used to tease her cat.

'I'm afraid I'm boring you with these details, but they have a certain importance. There were some more serious incidents, such as when some of the boys broke glass panes at her house, and when they threw filth in at the windows. She complained to the police any number of times. The constable called on me, asked me who'd done it.'

'Did you tell him?'

'I said they were all more or less mixed up in it, and that if only she'd stop trying to play at scarecrow by brandishing her stick, they'd probably calm down.'

'What happened on Tuesday?'

'Early in the afternoon, about half past one, Maria, a Polish woman with five children, who works as a char, went to Mère Birard's house, as she did every day. The windows were open, and from the school I heard her shrieks, the words she started to rattle off in her own language, as she does whenever she's upset. Her full name is Maria Smelker, and she came to the village when she was sixteen, as a farm servant; she's never been married. Her children have various fathers. It's said that at least two of them belong to the deputy-mayor. He hates me too, but that's another story. I'll tell you later about that.'

'So on Tuesday, about half past one, Maria cried for help?'

'Yes. I didn't leave the classroom, because I heard other people hurrying towards the old woman's house. After a short time I saw the doctor's little car go by.'

'You didn't go to have a look?'

'No. Some people are blaming me for that now, saying that the reason why I didn't move was because I knew what they'd found.'

'You couldn't leave the class, I suppose?'

'I could have done. I sometimes do, for a moment, to sign documents in the office at the *mairie*. Besides, I could have called my wife.'

'Is she a teacher?'

'She used to be.'

'In the country?'

'No. We were both teaching at Courbevoie, where we stayed for seven years. When I asked to be moved to the country, she handed in her resignation.'

'Why did you leave Courbevoie?'

'Because of my wife's health.'

The subject embarrassed him. He was answering less frankly.

'So, you didn't call your wife, as you sometimes do, and you stayed with your pupils.'

'Yes.'

'What happened next?'

'For more than an hour there was a great to-do. The village is usually very quiet. Noises can be heard a long way off. The hammering at Marchandon's smithy stopped. People were calling out to one another across the garden hedges. You know how it is when anything like that happens. So that the pupils shouldn't get excited, I went and closed the windows.'

'From the school windows you can see into Léonie Birard's house?'

'From one of the windows, yes.'

'What did you see?'

'To begin with, the village policeman; that surprised me, as he wasn't on speaking terms with his wife's aunt. And then Théo, the deputy-mayor, who must have been half drunk, as he usually is after ten o'clock in the morning. I saw the doctor, too, other neighbours, the whole lot bustling about in one room and looking down at the floor. Later on, the police lieutenant arrived from La Rochelle with two of his men. But I didn't know that until he knocked on the classroom door, and by that time he'd already put questions to a number of people.'

'He accused you of killing Léonie Birard?'

Gastin threw the chief-inspector a reproachful glance, as if to say:

'You know quite well it doesn't happen like that.'

And in rather flat tones, he explained:

'I noticed at once that he was looking strangely at me. The first thing he asked was:

' "Do you own a rifle, Gastin?"

'I said I didn't, but that Jean-Paul, my son, had one. That's another complicated story. You know what it's like with children, I expect. One morning one of them arrives at school with some marbles, and by next day all the boys are playing marbles, their pockets are bulging with them. Another day someone produces a kite, and kites are in fashion for weeks.

'Well, last autumn, someone or other brought a .22 rifle, and began shooting at sparrows with it. Within a month we had half a dozen guns of the same type. My boy wanted one for Christmas. I saw no reason to refuse. . . .'

Even the gun stirred memories in Maigret; the only difference was that his, in the old days, had been an air-gun and fired pellets that did no more than ruffle the birds' feathers.

'I told the police lieutenant that so far as I

knew, the gun was in Jean-Paul's room. He sent one of his men to find out. I ought to have asked the boy. It didn't occur to me. As it happened, the gun wasn't there, he'd left it in the hut in the kitchen garden, where I keep the wheelbarrow and the tools.'

'Léonie Birard was killed with a .22 rifle?'

'That's the most extraordinary thing. And it isn't all. The police lieutenant then asked me whether I'd left the classroom during that morning, and unfortunately I said no.'

'You had left?'

'For about ten minutes, soon after the morning break. When you're asked a question like that, you answer without thinking. Break finishes at ten o'clock. A little later—five minutes, perhaps—Piedbœuf, from Gros-Chêne farm, came to ask me to sign a paper he needed in order to draw his pension—he was disabled in the war. I usually have the *mairie* stamp in the classroom. That morning I hadn't got it, and I took the farmer along to the office. The children seemed quiet. As my wife isn't well, I went across the yard afterwards, to see if she needed anything.'

'Your wife has bad health?'

'It's chiefly nerves. In all, I may have been away for ten or fifteen minutes, more like ten than fifteen.'

'You didn't hear anything?'

'I remember Marchandon was shoeing a horse, because I heard the hammer clanging on the anvil and there was a smell of singed horn in

18

the air. The forge is next to the church, nearly opposite the school.'

'That's the time when Léonie Birard's supposed to have been killed?'

'Yes. They think someone must have shot her from one of the gardens, or from a window, when she was in her kitchen, at the back of the house.'

'She was killed by a .22 bullet?'

'That's the strangest thing of all. A bullet like that, fired from some way off, ought not to have done her much harm. But the fact is that it went into her head through the left eye and flattened against the skull.'

'Are you a good shot?'

'People think so, because they saw me at target-practice with my son during the winter. It happened three or four times, perhaps. Apart from that I've never touched a rifle, except on a fairground.'

'Didn't the lieutenant believe you?'

'He didn't definitely accuse me, but he seemed surprised that I hadn't admitted leaving the classroom. Afterwards, when I wasn't there, he questioned the children. He didn't tell me what the interrogation led to. He went back to La Rochelle. Next day—yesterday, that is—he came and settled down in my office, at the *mairie*, with Théo, the deputy-mayor, beside him.'

'Where were you then?'

'I was taking school. Out of thirty-two pupils, only eight had turned up. They sent for me twice to ask me the same questions, and the second time they made me sign my statement. They questioned my wife too. They asked her how long I'd stayed with her. They interrogated my son about the rifle.'

'But you weren't arrested.'

'I wasn't arrested yesterday. I feel sure I would have been today if I'd stayed at Saint-André. Just after dark, stones were thrown at our house. It upset my wife a lot.'

'You went off by yourself, leaving her there alone with your son?'

'Yes. I don't think they'll dare do anything to them. Whereas if they arrest me, they'll give me no chance to defend myself. Once I'm shut up I shan't be able to communicate with the outside world. No one will believe me. They'll do whatever they like with me.'

Again his forehead was damp with sweat and his linked fingers so tightly clenched that the blood could not circulate.

'Perhaps I was wrong? I thought that if I told you all about it, you would perhaps come and find out the truth. I'm not offering you money. I know that isn't what interests you. I swear to you, Inspector, that I didn't kill Léonie Birard.'

Maigret extended a hesitant hand towards the telephone, finally lifted the receiver.

'What's the name of your constabulary lieutenant?'

'Daniélou.'

'Hello! Get me the constabulary at La Rochelle. If Lieutenant Daniélou isn't there, see if you can find him at the *mairie* at Saint-André-

20

sur-Mer. Put him through to me in Lucas's office.'

He rang off, lit a pipe, and went over to stand facing the window. He was pretending to take no further notice of the schoolmaster, who had opened his mouth two or three times to thank him, but had not found the words.

The brilliant yellow glow in the air was gradually gaining over the blue, and the house-fronts across the Seine were changing to a creamy hue; the sun was reflected in an attic window somewhere at a distance.

'Was it you who asked for Saint André-sur-Mer, Chief?'

'Yes, Lucas. Stay here a minute.'

He went into the next-door office.

'Lieutenant Daniélou? This is Maigret, of Police Headquarters in Paris. I hear you're looking for someone?'

At the other end of the line, the constabulary officer was astounded.

'How did you know that already?'

'It's the schoolmaster?'

'Yes. I was a fool not to keep an eye on him. It never occurred to me that he'd try to give me the slip. He took the train to Paris last night, and . . .'

'You're bringing a charge against him?'

'A very serious one. And I have at least one damaging piece of evidence, acquired this morning.'

'Who from?'

'One of his pupils.'

'He saw something?'

'Yes.'

'What?'

'He saw the schoolmaster coming out of his tool-shed on Tuesday morning, about twenty past ten. And it was at a quarter past ten that the deputy-mayor heard a shot.'

'Have you asked the examining magistrate for an arrest warrant?'

'I was just off to La Rochelle to do it when you rang up. How did you know about it? Have the newspapers . . . ?'

'I haven't seen the newspapers. Joseph Gastin is in my office.'

There was a silence, then the lieutenant let out an:

'Ah!'

Whereupon he would doubtless have liked to ask a question. But he didn't do so. Maigret, for his part, was rather at a loss what to say. He had not made up his mind. If the sun had not been shining so brightly that morning, if the chief inspector hadn't, a little time ago, suddenly remembered Fourras, the oysters and the white wine, if he hadn't been over ten months without a chance of a holiday, even for three days, if . . .

'Hello? Are you still there?'

'Yes. What do you intend to do with him?'

'Bring him back to you.'

'Yourself?'

The tone was not enthusiastic, and the chief-inspector smiled.

'You may be sure I shall not dream of interfering in any way in your investigation.'

'You don't think he's . . .'

'I don't know. Perhaps he's guilty. Perhaps he isn't. Anyhow, I'm bringing him back to you.'

'Thank you. I'll be at the station.'

Back in his own office, he found Lucas gazing curiously at the schoolmaster.

'Wait another minute. I must have a word with the Chief.'

His work would allow him to take a few days off. When he came back, he asked Gastin:

'Is there an inn at Saint-André?'

'Yes, the *Bon Coin*, run by Louis Paumelle. The food's good, but the rooms don't have running water.'

'Are you going away, Chief?'

'Get my wife on the phone for me.'

All this was so unexpected that poor Gastin was dumbfounded, not yet daring to feel delighted.

'What did he say to you?'

'He'll probably arrest you the moment we get out of the train.'

'But . . . you're coming with me . . . ?'

Maigret nodded and took the telephone receiver which Lucas was holding out to him.

'That you, dear? Would you pack me a small suitcase, just underclothes and toilet things? . . . Yes. . . . Yes. . . . I don't know. . . . Three or four days, perhaps. . . .'

He added gleefully:

'I'm going to the seaside, in the Charentes. Right among the oysters and mussels. Meantime, I'll be lunching at a restaurant. See you presently. . . .'

He felt as though he were playing a joke on someone, like the small boys who had teased old Léonie Birard so much and for so long.

'Come along and have a bite with me,' he said finally to the schoolmaster, who got up and followed him as though in a dream.

2

A T Poitiers, while the train was in the station, the lights went up all at once along the platforms, but it wasn't dark yet. It was not until later, when they were crossing the open fields, that they noticed that night was falling, the windows of the scattered farm-houses starting to gleam like stars.

Then suddenly, a few miles outside La Rochelle, a light mist, which came not from the country but from the sea, began to mingle with the darkness, and the spark of a distant lighthouse shone for a moment.

There were two other people in the carriage, a man and a woman, who had been reading throughout the journey, looking up occasionally to exchange a few words. Most of the time, especially towards the end, Joseph Gastin had kept his weary eyes fixed on the chief-inspector.

The train crossed some points. Small houses slid past. The lines became more numerous, and at last they reached the platforms, the doors with their familiar notices, the people waiting, looking just like the people in previous stations. The moment the carriage door opened one felt a strong, cool breath from the empty blackness into which the rails seemed to vanish; and looking more attentively, one saw ships' masts and gently-rocking funnels, heard gulls screaming, recognized the smell of salt water and tar.

The three uniformed men standing near the entrance did not move. Lieutenant Daniélou was still young, with a little black moustache and thick eyebrows. Not until Maigret and his companion were within a few paces did he step forward, holding out his hand with a military gesture.

'Delighted, Chief-Inspector,' he said.

Maigret, noticing that one of the policemen was producing a pair of handcuffs from his pocket, murmured to the lieutenant:

'I don't think that's necessary.'

The lieutenant made a sign to his subordinate. A few heads had turned in their direction, not many. The passengers were trooping out, weighed down by their suitcases, now walking diagonally across the entrance hall.

'I have no intention of interfering in your inquiry in any way, Lieutenant. I hope you understand that. I'm not here in any official capacity.'

'I know. I discussed it with the examining magistrate.'

'I hope he isn't annoyed?'

'On the contrary, he's delighted that we'll be able to have your help. As things stand at present we can't do otherwise than put him under arrest.'

Joseph Gastin, three feet away, was pretending not to listen, could not help overhearing.

'Anyway, it's in his own interest. He'll be safer in prison than anywhere else. You know how people react in small towns and villages.'

All this was rather stilted. Maigret himself didn't feel too comfortable.

'Have you had dinner?'

'Yes, on the train.'

'Do you mean to spend the night at La Rochelle?'

'I'm told there's an inn at Saint-André.'

'May I offer you a drink?'

As Maigret neither accepted nor refused, the lieutenant turned to give orders to his men, who moved towards the schoolmaster. There was nothing the chief-inspector could say to Gastin, so he merely gave him a serious look.

'You heard. You'll have to go through with it,' he seemed to be saying apologetically. 'I'll do my best.'

Gastin gazed back at him, turned his head shortly afterwards for another glance, finally went out of the door, walking between the two constables.

'We'll do best to go to the buffet,' murmured Daniélou. 'Unless you'd like to come to my place?'

'Not tonight.'

A few travellers were eating in the ill-lit refreshment-room.

'What will you have?'

'I don't know. A brandy.'

They sat down in a corner, at a table which was still laid for dinner.

'You're not having anything to eat?' asked the waitress.

They shook their heads. Not until the drinks came did the lieutenant inquire, with an air of embarrassment:

'You think he's innocent?'

'I don't know.'

'Until the boy gave his evidence we were able to leave him at liberty. Unfortunately for him that evidence is conclusive, and the boy seems sincere, he has no reason to be lying.'

'When did he tell his story?'

'This morning, when I questioned the whole class for the second time.'

'He hadn't said anything yesterday?'

'He was scared. You'll see him. If you like I'll give you the file tomorrow morning, when I'm down there. I spend most of my time at the *mairie*.'

There was still a certain awkwardness. The lieutenant seemed overawed by the chief-inspector's massive bulk and by his reputation.

'You're accustomed to the things and people of Paris. I don't know if you're used to the atmosphere of our small villages.'

'I was born in a village. What about you?'

'At Toulouse.'

He managed to smile.

'Would you like me to drive you out there?'

'I think I'll find a taxi.'

'If you'd rather. There's a rank outside the station.'

They parted at the door of the taxi, which drove off along the seafront, and Maigret leant forward to make out the fishing-boats in the darkness of the harbour.

He was disappointed to have arrived at night. When they turned away from the sea and left the town, they drove through a stretch of country that looked like any other stretch, and soon, at the third village, the car stopped outside a lighted window.

'Is this it?'

'You said the *Bon Coin*, didn't you?'

A very stout man came to look out through the glass-panelled door, and, without opening it, watched while Maigret went to and fro, took out his suitcase, put it on the ground, paid the driver, finally walked towards the inn.

Men were playing cards in a corner. The inn smelt of wine and stew, and smoke hovered round the two lamps.

'Have you a room?'

Everyone was staring at him. A woman came to the kitchen door to look at him.

'For the night?'

'For two or three days, perhaps.'

They looked him up and down.

'Have you your identity card? The constables come here every morning and we have to keep the register up to date.'

The four men had stopped playing, were listening. Maigret, now standing at the counter, which was loaded with bottles, held out his card and the landlord put on his glasses to read it. When he looked up again, he gave a sly wink.

'So you're the famous inspector? My name's Paumelle, Louis Paumelle.'

He turned towards the kitchen and called:

'Thérèse! Take the inspector's suitcase up to the front room.'

Without paying special attention to the woman, who looked about thirty years old, Maigret had the impression that he'd seen her before somewhere. It only struck him later on, as with the people he used to see when he went past 'Purgatory'. He thought she had given a slight start, too.

'What will you take?'

'Whatever you have. A brandy, if you like.'

The others, for the sake of appearances, had returned to their game of *belote*.

'You've come because of Léonie?'

'Not officially.'

'Is it true the schoolmaster has been found in Paris?'

'He's in the prison at La Rochelle by now.'

It was hard to guess what Paumelle thought of the business. Although he was an innkeeper, he looked more like a peasant in his own farm.

'You don't think he did it?'

'I don't know.'

'I imagine that if you reckoned he was guilty you wouldn't have come all this way. Am I right?'

'Maybe.'

'Your very good health! There's a man here who heard the shot. Théo! It's true you heard the shot, isn't it?'

One of the card-players, sixty-five years old or perhaps more, his reddish hair going white here and there, cheeks unshaven, and his eyes shifty and spiteful, turned towards them.

'Why shouldn't I have heard it?'

'This is Inspector Maigret, who's come from Paris to . . .'

'The lieutenant told me about it.'

He did not get up nor give any greeting; he was holding his grimy cards between black-nailed fingers. Paumelle explained in an undertone:

'That's the deputy-mayor.'

And Maigret, in his turn, answered just as laconically:

'I know.'

'You mustn't take any notice. By this time of night . . .'

He made the gesture of emptying a glass.

'What about you, Ferdinand, what did you see?'

The man he called Ferdinand had only one arm. His complexion was ruddy-brown, that of a man who spent all his time out of doors.

'The postman,' explained Louis. 'Ferdinand Cornu. What did you see, Ferdinand?'

'Nothing at all.'

'You saw Théo in his garden.'

'I even brought him a letter.'

'What was he doing?'

'Planting out onions.'

'What time was it?'

'Just ten by the church clock. I could see the clock-face, above the houses. *Belote! Rebelote!* My nine beats it . . . Ace of spades, King of diamonds, takes all . . .'

He flung down his cards on the table where the glasses had left a wet circle, and glared defiantly at the other players.

'And to hell with people who come here to make trouble for us!' he added, getting to his feet. 'Pay up, Théo.'

His movements were clumsy, his gait unsteady. He took down his postman's cap from a peg and made for the door, growling out something indistinguishable.

'Is he like that every evening?'

'Pretty much.'

Louis Paumelle was about to fill the two glasses, and Maigret put out a hand to stop him.

'Not for the moment. . . . You won't be closing just yet, I suppose, and I've time for a stroll before going to bed?'

'I'll wait for you.'

He went out, amid dead silence. He found himself in a small open space, neither round nor square, with the dark mass of the church to his right, opposite him an unlighted shop, above whose window he could just decipher the words: *'Coopérative Charentaise'*.

There was a light in the house at the corner, a grey stone-built place. The light came from the first floor. Going up to the door, with its three steps, Maigret noticed a brass plate, lit a match, and read:

Xavier Bresselles: M.D.

For lack of something to do, and puzzled as to how to make a beginning, he was on the point of ringing the bell; then he shrugged his shoulders and reflected that the doctor was probably getting ready for bed.

Most of the houses were in darkness. He recognized the *mairie*, a one-storey building, by its flagstaff. It was a very small *mairie*, and above its courtyard a lamp was burning in a first-floor room of a building, probably the Gastins' house.

He went down the road, turned to the right, strolled past some houses and gardens, not long afterwards met the deputy-mayor, who was coming up from the opposite direction and gave a grunt by way of good night.

He could neither hear the sea nor get any glimpse of it. The slumbering village looked like any small country place and did not fit in with his expectation of oysters with white wine on a café terrace overlooking the ocean.

He was disappointed, for no definite reason. The lieutenant's greeting at the station had chilled him, to begin with. He could not blame the man. Daniélou knew the district, where he had most likely been stationed for some years. A crime had been committed, he had done his best to clear it up, and now Maigret had arrived from Paris, without warning, and appeared to think he was mistaken.

The examining magistrate must be annoyed too. Neither of them would dare to show their irritation, they would be polite, would put their files at his disposal. Maigret would still be a nuisance, interfering in what wasn't his business, and he began to wonder what had suddenly decided him to come on this trip.

He heard footsteps and voices, probably the other two *belote* players on their way home. Then, further on, a yellowish dog brushed against his leg and he gave a startled jump.

When he opened the door of the *Bon Coin* only one of the lamps was still burning, and the landlord, behind the counter, was putting away the glasses and bottles. He was wearing neither waistcoat nor jacket. His dark-coloured trousers were hanging very low on his bulging stomach, and his sleeves were rolled up, revealing fat, hairy arms.

'Made any discoveries?'

He was trying to be clever, doubtless thought himself the most important person in the village.

'A nightcap?'

'If you'll let this be my round.'

Ever since morning Maigret had been thirsting for some local white wine, but he asked for brandy again, feeling that this was not an hour to drink wine.

'Here's how!'

'I thought,' remarked the chief-inspector quietly, wiping his mouth, 'that Léonie Birard wasn't very popular.'

'She was the nastiest shrew on earth. She's dead. May the Lord have her soul, or more likely the devil, but she was undoubtedly the most unpleasant woman I've ever known. And I knew her when she still had pigtails down her back, and we went to school together. She was . . . wait a minute . . . three years older than me. That's right. I'm sixty-four. So she must have been sixty-seven. Even at twelve she was poisonous.'

'What I don't understand . . .' began Maigret.

'There are lots of things you won't understand, although you're such a smart chap, let me warn you.'

'I don't understand,' he began again, as though talking to himself, 'that although she was so much hated, everybody is so down on the schoolmaster. Because after all, even if he did kill her, one would rather expect . . .'

'That people would say, *Good riddance*! That's what you're thinking, isn't it?'

'More or less.'

'Yes, but you're forgetting that Léonie was a local woman.'

He refilled the glasses without being asked.

'It's like in a family, don't you see. Relations have the right to hate one another, and they certainly do. But if an outsider gets mixed up in it, things change. People loathed Léonie. They loathe Gastin and his wife still more.'

35

'His wife as well?'

'His wife particularly.'

'Why? What has she done?'

'Nothing—here.'

'Why : "here"?'

'Everything gets known in the end, even in a godforsaken village like ours. And we don't like to be landed with people who aren't wanted anywhere else. This isn't the first time the Gastins have been mixed up in some funny business.'

He was interesting to watch, as he stood leaning on his bar. He obviously wanted to talk, but after each sentence he was peering at Maigret to see what effect he was producing, ready to retreat, or even to contradict himself, like a peasant bargaining for a yoke of oxen in the market.

'Looks as though you'd come here without knowing anything?'

'Except that Léonie Birard was killed by a bullet through her left eye.'

'And you came all this way!'

He was laughing at Maigret, after his own fashion.

'You hadn't the curiosity to break the journey at Courbevoie?'

'Ought I to have?'

'You'd have heard a fine tale. It took a long time to get here. It's only about two years since we heard it, at Saint-André.'

'What tale?'

'Madame Gastin was a schoolteacher, together with her husband. They taught in the same school, she on the girls' side, he on the boys'.'

'I know.'

'Have you heard about Chevassou?'

'Who's Chevassou?'

'One of the municipal councillors there, a handsome fellow, tall and strong, with black hair and a southern accent. There was a Madame Chevassou too. One fine day when the children were going home from school, Madame Chevassou turned up in the street and shot at the schoolmistress, hitting her in the shoulder. Guess why? Because she'd discovered that her husband and Gastin's wife were having fun and games together. It seems she was acquitted. After which, the best thing the Gastins could do was to leave Courbevoie, and they suddenly developed a hankering for country air.'

'I don't see the connexion with the murder of Léonie Birard.'

'There may be no connexion.'

'From what you tell me, Joseph Gastin did nothing wrong.'

'He's a cuckold.'

Louis was grinning, thoroughly pleased with himself.

'He's not the only one, of course. This village is full of them. I wish you joy. One more drop?'

'No, thank you.'

'Thérèse will show you to your room. Tell her what time you'd like your hot water brought up.'

'Thank you. Good night.'

'Thérèse!'

She went ahead of him up a staircase with uneven steps, turned into a corridor with flower-patterned wallpaper, opened a door.

'Call me about eight,' he said.

She didn't move, but stood watching him as though she wanted to tell him something. He looked more closely at her.

'Haven't I met you before?'

'You remember?'

He didn't admit that it was a rather vague recollection.

'You won't talk about it here, will you?'

'Aren't you from the village?'

'Yes. But I went away when I was fifteen, to work in Paris.'

'Did you really work there?'

'For four years.'

'And then?'

'You saw me, so you know. Inspector Priollet will tell you I didn't take the pocket-book. It was my friend Lucille, and I didn't even know about it.'

A picture came back to his mind and he re-membered where he had seen her. One morning he had called in, as he often did, at the office of his colleague Priollet, head of the '*mondaine*' sec-tion, the Vice Squad. On a chair sat a dark, tou-sled-haired girl, dabbing at her eyes and snivelling. There was something about her pale, sickly face which had appealed to him.

'What's she done?' he had asked Priollet.

'The old story. A skivvy who's started picking up men along the Boulevard Sébastopol. Two days ago a shopkeeper from Béziers came to complain that his pocket had been picked, and was able, for once, to give us a fairly accurate description. Last night we caught her in a dance-hall in the Rue de Lappe.'

'It wasn't me!' stammered the girl between sobs. 'I swear to you on my mother's head that it wasn't me that took the pocket-book.'

The two men had exchanged winks.

'What do you think, Maigret?'

'Has she never been arrested before?'

'Not so far.'

'Where does she come from?'

'Somewhere in the Charentes.'

They often put on a little act of this kind.

'Have you found her girl friend?'

'Not yet.'

'Why not send this one home to her village?'

Priollet had turned solemnly to the girl.

'Would you like to go back to your village?'

'As long as they don't know about it there.'

It was strange to find her here now, five or six years older, still pale-faced, with big dark eyes that looked pleadingly at the chief-inspector.

'Is Louis Paumelle married?' he asked in a low voice.

'A widower.'

'Do you sleep with him?'

She nodded.

'Does he know what you were doing in Paris?'

'No. He mustn't find out. He's always promising to marry me. He's been promising for years, and sooner or later he's sure to make up his mind.'

'Thérèse!' called the landlord from the foot of the stairs.

'Just coming!'

And, to Maigret:

'You won't tell him?'

He shook his head, with an encouraging smile.

'Don't forget my hot water at eight o'clock.'

He was glad to have come across her again, because really with her he felt he was on familiar ground, and it was rather like meeting an old acquaintance.

He felt as though he knew the rest of them too, although he had only had a glimpse of them, because in his own village there had been a deputy-mayor who drank, there had been card-players—it wasn't *belote* in those days, it was piquet—a postman who thought himself somebody, and an innkeeper who knew everyone's secrets.

Their faces were still graven in his memory. But he had seen them with a child's eyes, and he realized, now, that he hadn't really known them.

While he was undressing he heard Paumelle coming upstairs, and then some thuds in the next room. Thérèse joined the innkeeper a little later and began undressing in her turn. Both were talking in low voices, like a married couple getting to bed, and the last sound was the creaking springs.

He had some difficulty in hollowing out a place

for himself in the two huge feather mattresses. He recognized the country smell of hay and damp and, either because of the feathers or because of the brandies in tumblers which he had drunk with the landlord, he began to sweat profusely.

Before daylight, sounds began to reach him through his sleep, including those of a herd of cows which went past the inn, with an occasional moo. The forge began work soon afterwards. Downstairs, someone was taking down the shutters. He opened his eyes, found the sun shining even more brilliantly than the day before in Paris, sat up and pulled on his trousers.

With slippers on his bare feet he went downstairs, found Thérèse in the kitchen, busy making coffee. She had put on a kind of dressing-gown with a sprigged pattern over her nightdress, and her legs were bare; she smelt of bed.

'It isn't eight yet. Only half past six. Would you like a cup of coffee? It'll be ready in five minutes.'

Paumelle came down in his turn, unwashed and unshaven, wearing bedroom slippers like the chief-inspector.

'I thought you didn't want to get up before eight o'clock.'

They drank their first cup of coffee in thick china bowls, standing up near the stove.

Outside the house there was a group of women dressed in black, carrying baskets and shopping-bags.

'What are they waiting for?' inquired Maigret.

'The bus. It's market day at La Rochelle.'

Hens could be heard cackling in crates.

'Who's taking school now?'

'Yesterday there was nobody. This morning they're expecting a substitute from La Rochelle. He's to come on the bus. He'll sleep here, in the back room, as you've got the front one.'

He was up in his room again when the bus stopped in the square and he saw a timid-looking young man get out, carrying a big gladstone-bag; this must be the schoolmaster.

The crates were piled on the roof of the bus. The women packed themselves into it. Thérèse knocked on his door.

'Your hot water!'

Casually, without looking at her, he asked:

'Are you another who thinks Gastin killed Léonie?'

Before replying she glanced towards the half-open door.

'I don't know,' she said in a very low tone.

'You don't think so?'

'It doesn't seem like him. But they all want it to be him, you understand?'

The chief thing he was beginning to understand was that, for no reason, he had taken a difficult, if not impossible, job.

'Who stood to benefit by the old woman's death?'

'I don't know. They say she disinherited her niece for getting married.'

'Who'll get her money?'

'Some charity, perhaps. She changed her mind

so often! . . . Or it might be Maria, the Polish woman. . . .'

'Is it true she's had one or two children by the deputy-mayor?'

'Maria? So they say. He often goes to see her, and sometimes stays for the night.'

'In spite of the children?'

'That doesn't worry Maria. Everybody goes there.'

'Paumelle too?'

'I expect he did when she was younger. She's not very tempting nowadays.'

'How old is she?'

'About thirty. She takes no trouble about herself, and her house is worse than a pigsty.'

'Thérèse!' came the landlord's voice, as on the previous evening.

Better not detain her, Paumelle didn't seem to like it. Was he perhaps jealous? Or merely anxious that she shouldn't tell too much?

When Maigret went downstairs, the young schoolmaster was having breakfast and looked inquisitively at him.

'What will you have, Inspector?'

'Have you any oysters?'

'Not at neap-tide.'

'Will that last much longer?'

'Another five or six days.'

Ever since Paris he'd been wanting to eat oysters washed down with white wine, and it looked as though he wouldn't get any all the time he was here.

'There's soup. Or we can do you some ham and eggs.'

He ate nothing at all, drank another cup of coffee, standing at the open door and looking at the sunlit square and at two dark figures moving about in the '*Coopérative Charentaise*'.

He was wondering whether to ask for a glass of white wine all the same, to take away the taste of the abominable coffee, when a cheerful voice exclaimed, close beside him:

'Inspector Maigret?'

It was a small, thin, lively man, whose expression was youthful although he must be over forty. He held out his hand with a cordial gesture.

'Dr. Bresselles!' he introduced himself. 'The lieutenant told me yesterday that you were expected. I came along before surgery, to know if I could help you. An hour from now my waiting-room will be packed.'

'Will you have something to drink?'

'In my house, if you'll come, it's next door.'

'I know.'

Maigret followed him to the grey stone house. All the other houses in the village were colour-washed, some in harsh white, others in a creamier shade, and the pink roofs gave the whole place a very gay appearance.

'Come in! What would you like to drink?'

'Ever since I left Paris I've been longing for oysters and local white wine,' confessed Maigret. 'But I've already discovered that I shall have to do without the oysters.'

'Armande!' he called, crossing to the door.

'Bring up a bottle of white wine. From the red bin.'

He explained:

'That's my sister. She's been keeping house for me since my wife died. I have two boys, one at Niort, at the *Lycée*, the other's doing his military service. What do you think of Saint-André?'

Everything seemed to amuse him.

'I'm forgetting you've not seen much of it yet. Just wait! By way of a sample, you have that scoundrel Paumelle, who was a farm-hand and married the owner of the *Bon Coin* when her husband died. She was twenty years older than Louis. She liked her little drop to drink. So as she was fiendishly jealous and the money was hers, he killed her by encouraging her weakness. See what I mean? He did his best to fill her up with drink, and by the time lunch was over she often had to go upstairs to bed. She held out for seven years, with a liver as hard as stone, and in the end he was able to give her a handsome funeral. Since then, he's been going to bed with his servants. One after another they left, till it came to Thérèse, who seems to be sticking it out.'

The sister came in, timid and colourless, carrying a tray with a bottle and two glasses, and Maigret thought she looked like a priest's housekeeper.

'My sister. Inspector Maigret.'

She went out backwards, and this, too, seemed to amuse the doctor.

'Armande has never married. I'm inclined to

think she's been waiting all her life for me to be a widower. Now she has her own house at last, and can spoil me as she would have spoilt a husband.'

'What do you think of Gastin?'

'He's pathetic.'

'Why?'

'Because he does his best, despairingly, and people who do their best are pathetic. He gets no thanks from anyone. He struggles away to teach something to a bunch of snotty little boys whom their parents would rather keep at home on the farm. He even tried to get them to wash. I remember the day he sent one of them home because his head was lousy. A quarter of an hour later the father turned up, furious, and they nearly came to blows.'

'His wife is an invalid?'

'Your very good health! She isn't really an invalid, but she isn't very well either. I've learnt not to put too much confidence in medicine, you know. Madame Gastin pines. She's ashamed. She blames herself, day in and day out, for ruining her husband's career.'

'Because of Chevassou?'

'You know about that? Yes, because of Chevassou. She must have been really in love with him. What's called a devouring passion. You'd never think it to look at her, for she's an insignificant little woman; she and her husband are as like as two peas. Maybe that's the real trouble. They're too much alike. Chevassou, who's a big brute full of vitality, a kind of satisfied bull, did what he liked with her. Her right arm still hurts her now and then, it's remained a bit stiff.'

'How did she get on with Léonie Birard?'

'They never saw each other except through their windows, across the courtyard and the gardens, and Léonie put out her tongue at her now and then, as she did at everyone. What strikes me as most extraordinary in this business is that Léonie, whom one would have imagined to be indestructible, was killed by a little bullet fired from a child's rifle. And that isn't all. There are some incredible coincidences. The left eye, the one that was hit, was her bad eye; she'd always been slightly wall-eyed, and she hadn't been able to see with it for years. What do you say to that?'

The doctor raised his glass. The wine had greenish lights in it, it was dry and light, with a strong local flavour.

'Your good health! They'll all try to put spokes in your wheel. Don't believe a word they say, whether it's the parents or the children. Come and see me whenever you like, and I'll do my utmost to help.'

'You don't like them?'

The doctor's eyes began to sparkle with laughter, and he retorted emphatically:

'I adore them! They're quite crazy!'

3

T H E door of the *mairie* stood open into a corridor
on whose recently whitewashed walls various
official notices were fixed with drawing-pins.
Some of the smaller ones, such as the announce-
ment of a special meeting of the Council, were
written in pen and ink, with the headings in
round-hand, probably by the schoolmaster. The
floor was grey-tiled, the woodwork painted in
grey also. The door on the left presumably led
into the council-room, with its bust of Marianne
and its flag, while the right-hand door, which
stood ajar, gave into the secretary's office.

The room was empty; it smelt of stale cigar-
smoke; Lieutenant Daniélou, who had made the
office his headquarters for the past two days,
had not yet arrived.

Opposite the street entrance, at the far end of
the passage, a double door stood open on to the

courtyard, in the middle of which grew a lime-tree. To the right of this yard, the low building, of which three windows were visible, was the school, with rows of boys' and girls' heads and, standing up, the outline of the substitute teacher whom Maigret had seen at the inn.

There was a monastic hush over all this, and only the clang of the blacksmith's hammer could be heard. Beyond, there were hedges and gardens, with the tender green of budding leaves on lilac bushes, white and yellow houses, an open window here and there.

Maigret turned left, towards the Gastins' two-storey house. As he was about to knock on the door it opened, and he found himself on the threshold of a kitchen where a small, spectacled boy was seated at the oilcloth-covered table, bending over an exercise-book.

It was Madame Gastin who had opened the door to him. Looking out of the window, she had seen him in the yard, glance around, come slowly forward.

'I heard yesterday that you were coming,' she said, standing aside to let him pass. 'Come in, Inspector. If you only knew how relieved I feel!'

She wiped her wet hands on her apron, turned towards her son, who had not looked up and seemed to be ignoring the visitor.

'Aren't you going to say how do you do to Inspector Maigret, Jean-Paul?'

'How do you do.'

'Run along up to your room now.'

The kitchen was small but, even at this early

hour, meticulously clean, without a trace of untidiness. Young Gastin picked up his book without protest, went out into the corridor and up the stairs to the floor above.

'Come this way, Inspector.'

They crossed the passage in their turn, went into a room which served as a parlour and was doubtless never used. There was an upright piano against one wall, a round, massive oak table, arm-chairs with lace antimacassars, photographs on the walls, ornaments all over the place.

'Please sit down.'

The house had four rooms, all tiny, and it made Maigret feel too tall and too broad, in addition to which he had had, ever since he came in, the impression of having suddenly entered an unreal world.

He had been warned that Madame Gastin was the same type as her husband, but he had never imagined that she was so much like him that they might practically have been taken for brother and sister. Her hair was of the same indeterminate colour, already thinning too, the middle of her face was, as it were, thrust forward, and she had pale, short-sighted eyes. And the child, too, was like a caricature of both his parents combined.

Was he trying, from upstairs, to overhear the conversation, or had he gone back to his exercise-book? He was only about twelve and already he looked like a little old man, or, to be more exact, like a being with no definite age.

'I kept him away from school,' explained Madame Gastin as she closed the door. 'I thought it was better. You know how cruel children are.'

If Maigret had remained standing he would almost have filled the room, and he now sat motionless in an arm-chair, signed to his hostess to sit down too, because it made him feel tired to see her standing.

She was as ageless as her son. He knew she was only thirty-four, but he had seldom seen a woman who had so completely discarded every feminine touch. Under her dress, whose colour was undefinable, her body was thin, tired; there was a hint of breasts that hung down like empty pockets, and her shoulders were already slightly rounded, her face, instead of being tanned by the country sunshine, had turned grey. Even her voice sounded washed-out!

But she was doing her best to smile, put forward a timid hand to touch Maigret's arm as she said:

'I'm so grateful to you for having confidence in him!'

He couldn't reply that he didn't know yet, couldn't confess to her that it was because of the first spring sunshine in Paris, of a memory of oysters and white wine, that he had suddenly decided to come.

'If you knew how much I blame myself, Inspector! Because what is happening is all my fault. I've ruined his life and the boy's. I'm doing my best to make up for it. I try so hard, you know. . . .'

He felt as uncomfortable as if he had come

unawares into a house where someone he didn't know had died, and was at a loss for words. All of a sudden he was in a world apart, which didn't belong to the village in the centre of which he was now ensconced.

These three, Gastin, his wife and their son, belonged to a race so different that the chief-inspector could understand the peasants' mistrust.

'I don't know how it will all end,' she was continuing after a sigh, 'but I can't believe that the law will condemn an innocent man. He's such an exceptional character! You've met him, but you don't know him. Tell me, how was he, last night?'

'Very well. Very calm.'

'Is it true they handcuffed him, on the station platform?'

'No. He went freely between the two constables.'

'Were there any people there to see him?'

'It was all done discreetly.'

'Do you think there's anything he needs? His health isn't good. He's never been very strong.'

She was not crying. She must have wept so much in her life that there were no more tears left in her. Just above her head, to the right of the window, hung the photograph of a young woman who was almost plump, and Maigret could not tear his eyes away from this, wondering if she had really looked like that, with laughing eyes and dimpled cheeks even.

'You're looking at my picture when I was young?'

There was another, of Gastin, to match it. He had scarcely changed at all, except that in those days he had longish hair, like an artist, as people used to say, and no doubt he used to write poems.

'Have you been told?' she asked softly, after glancing at the door.

And he could feel that that was what she chiefly wanted to talk about, it had been in her mind ever since she had been told he was coming, it was the only thing that mattered to her.

'You mean about what happened at Courbevoie?'

'Yes, about Charles . . .'

She stopped short and blushed, as though the name were taboo.

'Chevassou?'

She nodded.

'I'm still wondering how it could ever have happened. I've been so miserable, Inspector! And I do wish someone would explain to me! I'm not a bad woman, you know. I met Joseph when I was only fifteen, and I knew at once that he was the man I should marry. We planned our lives together. We both decided to take up teaching.'

'Was it he who gave you the idea?'

'I think so. He's cleverer than I am. He's a very exceptional man. People don't always realize that, because he's too modest. We took our degrees the same year and got married; thanks to a cousin who had influence, we managed to get appointments at Courbevoie together.'

'Do you think that has any connexion with what happened here on Tuesday?'

She looked at him in surprise. He would have done better not to interrupt her, for she lost the thread of what she was saying.

'It's all my fault.'

She frowned, anxious to explain.

'If it hadn't been for what happened at Courbevoie, we shouldn't have come here. People thought well of Joseph there. Their ideas are more modern, you know. He was getting on. He had good prospects.'

'And you?'

'I had, too. He used to help me, give me advice. And then, from one day to the next, it was as though I'd gone mad. I still can't understand what took possession of me. I didn't want it. I fought against it. I told myself I'd never do such a thing. And then, when Charles was there . . .'

She blushed again, stammered, as though it were an offence to Maigret himself to refer to the man:

'I beg your pardon. . . . When he was there I couldn't resist. I don't think it was love, because I love Joseph, I always have loved him. It was like a sort of fever, and I lost all thought of anything else, even of our boy, who was quite a baby. I was ready to leave him, Inspector. I really thought of leaving them both, going off somewhere, anywhere. . . . Can you understand it?'

He hadn't the courage to tell her that she had doubtless never had any sexual enjoyment with her husband and that her story was a commonplace one. She needed to believe that her adventure had been exceptional, she needed to lament, to be filled with remorse, to regard herself as the lowest of women.

'You are a Catholic, Madame Gastin?'

He was touching on another sensitive point.

'I was, like my parents, until I met Joseph. He only believes in science and progress. He loathes priests.'

'You stopped being a practising Catholic?'

'Yes.'

'Since those things happened, you haven't been back to church?'

'I couldn't. I feel as though I should be betraying him again. Besides, what would be the good! During our first few years here I did hope we were beginning a new life. The people looked at us suspiciously, as country people always do. But I felt sure that one day they would learn to appreciate my husband's qualities. Then, I don't know how, they found out about Courbevoie, and after that even the children didn't respect him any more. I told you it is all my fault . . .'

'Did your husband have arguments with Léonie Birard?'

'Now and then. As secretary of the *mairie*. She was a woman who always made difficulties. There were questions of pensions to be settled. Joseph is strict. He refuses to go beyond his duty, he'll never sign a false certificate to please anybody.'

'Did she know your story?'

'Yes, everyone did.'

'She used to put out her tongue at you too?'

'And make filthy remarks when I went past her house. I used to avoid going that way. Not only did she put her tongue out, but sometimes, when she saw me at the window, she'd turn round and pull up her skirts. I beg your pardon. One would hardly believe it, of such an old woman. She was like that. But it would never have occurred to Joseph to kill her, all the same. He'd never kill anyone. You've seen him. He's a gentle creature, who'd like everyone to be happy.'

'Tell me about your son.'

'What is there to tell you? He takes after his father. He's a quiet, studious boy, very advanced for his age. The only reason he isn't head of the class is that then my husband would be accused of favouritism. Joseph gives him lower marks than he deserves, on purpose.'

'Doesn't the boy object to that?'

'He understands. We've explained to him why it has to be that way.'

'Does he know about the Courbevoie business?'

'We've never mentioned it to him. But the other boys do. He pretends to know nothing about it.'

'Does he ever go to play with the others?'

'He used to at first. The last two years, since the village became openly hostile to us, he's preferred to stay at home. He reads a great deal. I'm teaching him the piano. He already plays very well for his age.'

The window was shut, and Maigret was beginning to feel stifled, to wonder whether he hadn't suddenly been caught fast, in an old photograph-album.

'Your husband came into the house on Tuesday morning, soon after ten o'clock?'

'Yes. I think so. I've been asked that so often, in all kinds of ways, as though they were determined to make me contradict myself, that I'm no longer positive about anything. He usually comes to the kitchen for a moment during the break, and helps himself to a cup of coffee. I'm generally upstairs at that time.'

'He doesn't drink wine?'

'Never. He doesn't smoke either.'

'On Tuesday, didn't he come in during the break?'

'He says he didn't. So I said the same, because he always tells the truth. Then they maintained he'd come in later.'

'You denied that?'

'I was speaking in good faith, Monsieur Maigret. Some time afterwards, I remembered finding his empty coffee-bowl on the kitchen table. I don't know whether it was during break or later, that he came.'

'He could have gone to the tool-shed without your seeing him?'

'The room I was in upstairs doesn't overlook the kitchen-garden.'

'You could see Léonie Birard's house?'

'If I'd looked that way, yes.'

'You didn't hear the shot?'

'I didn't hear anything. The window was shut.

I feel the cold a great deal. I always have. And even in summer I shut the windows during the break, because of the noise.'

'You tell me the local people don't like your husband. I'd like to get that clearer. Is there anyone in the village who particularly dislikes him?'

'Indeed there is. The deputy-mayor.'

'Théo?'

'Théo Coumart, yes, who lives just behind us. Our gardens are end to end. First thing in the morning he begins to drink white wine in his cellar, where there's always a barrel on tap. By ten or eleven o'clock he's at Louis's, and he goes on drinking till evening.'

'Hasn't he any work?'

'His parents owned a big farm. He's never done a stroke of work in his life. One afternoon last winter, when Joseph had gone to La Rochelle with Jean-Paul, he came into the house, at about half past four. I was upstairs, changing. I heard heavy footsteps on the stairs. It was he. He was drunk. He pushed the door open and began to laugh. Then, all of a sudden, as though this were a brothel, he tried to push me over on to the bed. I grabbed at his face, giving him a long scratch down his nose. It bled. He began to swear, shouting that a woman like me had no business to put on airs. I opened the window and threatened to call for help. I was in my underclothes. At last he went away, chiefly because of his bleeding face, I think. He's never spoken to me since.

'He's the village leader. The mayor, Monsieur Rateau, owns a mussel-bed; he's occupied all the time with his business, and only comes to the *mairie* for Council meetings.

'Théo arranges the elections just as he likes, does good turns to people, is always ready to sign any paper they want . . .'

'You don't know whether he was in his garden on Tuesday morning, as he makes out?'

'If he says so it's probably true, because other people must have seen him. Though of course if he asked them to oblige him by telling a lie, they wouldn't hesitate to do it.'

'Would you mind if I had a little chat with your son?'

She stood up resignedly, and opened the door.

'Jean-Paul, come down, will you?'

'Why?' asked the voice from upstairs.

'Inspector Maigret wants a word with you.'

Hesitant steps were heard. The little boy appeared, carrying a book, and stood waiting in the doorway, with a suspicious expression on his face.

'Come in, my boy. You're not afraid of me, I take it?'

'I'm not afraid of anyone.'

He spoke in almost the same toneless voice as his mother.

'You were at school on Tuesday morning?'

He glanced from the chief-inspector to his mother, as though uncertain whether he should answer even such a harmless question.

'Go on, Jean-Paul. The inspector's on our side.'

59

She looked at Maigret as though silently apologizing for this statement. But she could elicit no more than a nod from the boy.

'What happened after break?'

The same silence. Maigret was becoming a monument of patience.

'You want your father to come out of prison, don't you, and the real murderer to be arrested?'

It was hard to read the expression in his eyes, through the thick lenses of his spectacles. He did not look aside, but stared his questioner straight in the face, without the slightest flicker of his pinched features.

'Just now,' the chief-inspector went on, 'I don't know what people are saying. Some little thing, that seems quite unimportant, may give me a clue. How many of you are there in the school?'

'Answer, Jean-Paul.'

Reluctantly, he said:

'Thirty-two altogether.'

'What do you mean by "altogether"?'

'Seniors and juniors. The whole lot whose names are on the list.'

His mother explained:

'There are always some who are away. At times, especially in the summer, only about fifteen come, and we can't always be sending constables to their homes.'

'Have you any school-friends?'

He replied shortly: 'No.'

'Not one friend, among the village children?'

The answer came with an air of defiance:

'I'm the schoolmaster's son.'

'Is that why they don't like you?'

He didn't reply.

'What do you do in the breaks?'

'Nothing.'

'You don't come to see your mother?'

'No.'

'Why not?'

'Father doesn't let me.'

Madame Gastin explained again:

'He doesn't want to make any difference between his boy and the others. If Jean-Paul came here during break there would be no reason why the forester's boy, or the butcher's, for instance, shouldn't cross the road to their own homes.'

'I see. Do you remember what your father was doing on Tuesday during the break?'

'No.'

'Doesn't he keep an eye on the boys?'

'Yes.'

'Standing in the middle of the playground?'

'Sometimes.'

'He didn't come in here?'

'I don't know.'

He had seldom questioned anyone so recalcitrant. If he had been dealing with a grown-up person he would probably have lost his temper, and Madame Gastin, feeling this, stood protectively beside her son, laid a conciliatory hand on his shoulder.

'Answer the inspector politely, Jean-Paul.'

'I'm not being rude.'

'At ten o'clock you all went back into the classroom. Did your father go to the blackboard?'

Through the window-curtains he could see a section of the board, with words written on it in chalk, in the opposite building.

'Perhaps.'

'What lesson was it?'

'Grammar.'

'Did someone knock at the door?'

'Perhaps.'

'Aren't you sure? Didn't you see your father go out?'

'I don't know.'

'Now listen. When the teacher leaves the class, the boys generally begin jumping up, chattering, playing the fool.'

Jean-Paul said nothing.

'Is that what happened on Tuesday?'

'I don't remember.'

'You didn't leave the room?'

'What for?'

'You might have gone to the lavatory, for instance. I see it's in the yard.'

'I didn't go there.'

'Who went to look out of the window?'

'I don't know.'

By this time Maigret was standing up, and his fists, in his pockets, were tightly clenched.

'Now listen . . .'

'I don't know anything. I didn't see anything. I've nothing to tell you.'

And the boy suddenly rushed out of the room and up the stairs; they heard him, up above, shutting his door.

'You mustn't be cross with him, Inspector. Put

yourself in his place. Yesterday the lieutenant questioned him for over an hour, and when he got home he didn't say a word to me, went and lay down on his bed and stayed there till it was dark, with his eyes wide open.'

'Is he fond of his father?'

She didn't quite understand the question.

'I mean, has he a particular affection or admiration for his father? Or does he prefer you, for instance? Is it in you that he confides, or in his father.'

'He doesn't confide in anyone. He's undoubtedly fonder of me than of his father.'

'How did he behave when your husband was accused?'

'Just as you've seen him now.'

'He didn't cry?'

'I've never seen him cry since he was a baby.'

'How long has he had that gun?'

'We gave it to him for Christmas.'

'Does he often use it?'

'He goes off alone now and then, with his gun on his arm, like a sportsman, but I don't think he often fires it. Two or three times he pinned a paper target to the lime-tree in the yard, but my husband explained that he was wounding the tree.'

'If he'd left the classroom on Tuesday while your husband was away, I suppose the other boys would have noticed it?'

'Certainly.'

'And they would have said so.'

'You can't have thought that Jean-Paul . . . ?'

'I have to think of every possibility. Who is the boy who claims to have seen your husband come out of the tool-shed?'

'Marcel Sellier.'

'Whose son is he?'

'His father is the village policeman, who's also the ironmonger, the electrician and the plumber. He mends roofs too, when it's needed.'

'How old is Marcel Sellier?'

'The same age as Jean-Paul, to within two or three months.'

'Does he work well?'

'The best of them all, with my son. So as not to seem to favour Jean-Paul, my husband always puts Marcel at the head of the class. His father is intelligent too, and hard-working. They're a good kind of people, I think. Are you very cross with him?'

'With whom?'

'Jean-Paul. He was almost rude to you. And here am I, not even offering you anything to drink. Won't you have something?'

'Thank you, but the lieutenant must have arrived by now, and I promised to go and see him.'

'You'll keep on helping us?'

'Why do you ask me that?'

'Because if I were you, I think I should have lost heart. You've come so far, and what you find here is so uninspiring. . . .'

'I'll do my best.'

He went towards the door, to prevent her from seizing his hands in a gesture he could feel she was on the point of making, and kissing them, perhaps. He was eager to get out, to feel the fresh air on his face, to hear sounds other than the tired voice of the schoolmaster's wife.

'I shall be coming to see you again, I expect.'

'You don't think there's anything he needs?'

'If there is, I'll let you know.'

'Oughtn't he to choose a lawyer?'

'There's no need to do that yet.'

While he was crossing the yard without looking back, the double, glass-paned doors of the school were thrown open and a pack of children rushed out, yelling. Some of them stopped dead on seeing him, knowing doubtless from their parents who he was, and stared.

They were of all ages, from shrimps of six to big lads of fourteen or fifteen, who looked almost grown-up already. There were girls, too, who collected in one corner of the yard, as though taking refuge from the boys.

At the far end of the corridor, where both doors were open, Maigret saw the car from the constabulary. He stopped at the secretary's office and knocked. Daniélou's voice said:

'Come in!'

The lieutenant, who had taken off his belt and unbuttoned his tunic, stood up to shake hands. He was sitting in Gastin's chair, papers spread in front of him, *mairie* stamps lying all round. Because she was seated in a dark corner, Maigret did not immediately notice a stout girl with a baby in her arms.

'Sit down, Chief-Inspector. I'll be with you in a moment. I thought it would be a good thing to send for all the witnesses again and go right through the interrogations a second time.'

Doubtless because the chief-inspector had come to Saint-André.

'A cigar?'

'No, thank you. I only smoke a pipe.'

'I was forgetting.'

The lieutenant himself smoked very black cigars, which he chewed as he talked.

'Excuse me.'

And, turning to the girl:

'You say she promised to leave you all she had, including the house?'

'Yes. She promised.'

'Before witnesses?'

She didn't seem to understand what this meant. In fact she didn't seem to understand anything much; she looked as though she might be the village idiot.

She was a big, stolid, manly girl, wearing a black dress that someone must have given her, and there were wisps of hay in her untidy hair. She stank. The baby, too, smelt dirty and unkempt.

'When did she give this promise?'

'A long time ago.'

Her large eyes were of an almost transparent blue and she was frowning with the effort to understand what was wanted of her.

'What do you call a long time? A year?'

'Maybe a year.'

'Two years?'

'Maybe.'

'How long have you been working for Léonie Birard?'

'Wait a minute. . . . After I had my second baby. . . . No, the third. . . .'

'How old is he now?'

Her lips moved, as though in church, while she made a mental calculation.

'Five.'

'Where is he now?'

'At home.'

'How many of them are there at home?'

'Three. I've got one here, and the eldest is at school.'

'Who's looking after them?'

'Nobody.'

The two men exchanged glances.

'So you've been working for Léonie Birard for about five years. Did she promise at once that she'd leave you her money?'

'No.'

'After two years, or three?'

'Yes.'

'Was it two, or three?'

'I don't know.'

'Didn't she sign a paper?'

'I don't know.'

'You don't know either why she made you that promise?'

'To annoy her niece. She told me so.'

'Used her niece to come and visit her?'

'Never.'

'She's Madame Sellier, the village policeman's wife, isn't she?'

'That's right.'

'Didn't the policeman ever come to see her either?'

'Yes.'

'They had quarrelled?'

'Yes.'

'Why did he come to see her?'

'To threaten to summons her for throwing her rubbish out of the window.'

'Did they get angry?'

'They shouted insults at each other.'

'Were you fond of your employer?'

She gazed at him with her round eyes, as though the notion of being fond of anyone, or the contrary, had never occurred to her.

'I don't know.'

'Was she kind to you?'

'She used to give me left-overs.'

'Left-overs from what?'

'Food. And her old dresses too.'

'Did she pay you regularly?'

'Not much.'

'What do you mean by not much?'

'Half what other women give me to work for them. But she took me every afternoon. So that . . .'

'Have you heard her quarrelling with other people?'

'With nearly everyone.'

'In her own home?'

'She never left home lately; she used to shout things at people through the window.'

'What things?'

'Things they'd done and didn't want known about.'

'So everyone hated her?'

'I think so.'

'Did anyone hate her especially, enough to want to kill her?'

'Must have, seeing she was killed.'

'But you haven't the faintest idea who can have done it?'

'I thought you knew.'

'What do you mean?'

'Well, you've arrested the schoolmaster.'

'You think he did it?'

'I don't know.'

'Do you mind if I ask a question?' intervened Maigret, turning to the lieutenant.

'By all means.'

'Is Théo, the deputy-mayor, the father of one or more of your children?'

She was not offended, seemed to be pondering.

'He may be. I'm not sure.'

'Did he get along well with Léonie Birard?'

She thought again.

'Same as the rest.'

'He knew she'd promised to remember you in her will?'

'I told him.'

'What was his reaction?'

She didn't understand the word. He tried again:

'What did he say to that?'

'He told me to ask her for a paper.'

'You did so?'

'Yes.'

'When?'

'A long time ago.'

'Did she refuse?'

'She said everything was arranged.'

'When you found her dead, what did you do?'

'I called out.'

'Straight away?'

'As soon as I saw there was blood. At first I thought she'd fainted.'

'You didn't hunt through her drawers?'

'What drawers?'

Maigret signed to the lieutenant that he had finished. The latter stood up.

'Thank you, Maria. If I need you again, I'll send for you.'

'Didn't she sign any paper?' inquired the woman, pausing near the door, with her baby in her arms.

'We've found nothing so far.'

Turning her back on them, she grumbled:

'I might have known she'd cheat me.'

They saw her going past the window, talking to herself with a discontented air.

4

THE lieutenant sighed, as though apologizing:
'You see? I do my best.'

And that was undoubtedly true. He was all
the more conscientious now that there was a
witness to his investigation, someone from the
famous Police Headquarters, who must seem
very impressive to him.

His was a curious story. He came of a well-
known family at Toulouse, and on the insistence
of his parents he had gone to the Polytechnique,
where he acquitted himself more than credit-
ably. And then, instead of choosing between the
army and a business career, he had opted for
the constabulary and decided to read law for two
years.

He had a pretty wife, who also came of a good
family, and they were one of the most popular
couples at La Rochelle.

He was doing his best to appear at ease in the greyish room in the *mairie*, into which the sun was not yet shining, so that, in contrast with the brightness outside, it was almost dark.

'It's not easy to discover what they think!' he remarked, lighting another cigar.

Six .22 rifles were leaning against the wall in a corner of the room; four of them were exactly alike and one was of an older type, with a carved butt.

'I think I've got them all. If there are any more around, my men will find them this morning.'

From the mantelpiece he picked up what looked like a cardboard pill-box, and took out a flattened scrap of lead.

'I've inspected this carefully. I studied ballistics at one time, and we've no expert at La Rochelle. It's a lead bullet, of the type sometimes called "soft", which squashes flat as soon as it hits anything, even a pinewood plank. So it's no use looking it over for the kind of marks one finds on other bullets, which often help to identify the actual weapon used.'

Maigret nodded his understanding.

'You're familiar with the .22 rifle, Chief-Inspector?'

'More or less.'

Less rather than more, for he could not recall any crime committed in Paris with such a weapon.

'Two types of cartridge can be used in it, short or long. The short ones have a small range, but the long .22 can hit its target at over a hundred and fifty yards.'

On the veined marble mantelpiece other scraps of lead, some twenty in all, lay in a little heap.

'Yesterday we made some tests with these different rifles. The bullet which hit Léonie Birard is a long .22, of the same weight as those we fired.'

'The cartridge-case hasn't been found?'

'My men have been over the gardens, behind the house, with a fine-tooth comb. They'll make another search this afternoon. It's not impossible that whoever fired the shot picked up the case. What I'm trying to explain is that we have very few definite clues.'

'Have all these guns been used recently?'

'Fairly recently. It's difficult to be quite sure, because the boys don't bother to clean and oil them after use. The medical report, which I've got here, doesn't help much, either, because the doctor couldn't say, even approximately, from what distance the shot was fired. It might be fifty yards or it might be over a hundred.'

Maigret, standing near the window, was filling his pipe and listening with only half an ear. In the opposite building, next to the church, he could see a man with tangled black hair, shoeing a horse whose hoof was being held by a younger lad.

'I've been over all the different possibilities with the examining magistrate. The first thing we thought of, strange as it may seem, was that it might have been an accident. There's something so incredible about the crime, there was so little chance of killing the old woman with a

.22 bullet, that we wondered whether she hadn't been shot by pure chance. Somebody in one of the gardens might have been taking pot-shots at sparrows, as the kids often do. One hears of stranger coincidences. You see what I mean?'

Maigret nodded. The lieutenant had an almost childish desire for his approval, and his good intentions were touching.

'That's what we called the pure and simple accident theory. If Leónie Birard had been killed at any other time of day, or on a holiday, or in another part of the village, we should probably have been satisfied with that, for it's the most plausible. But when she was killed the children were at school.'

'All of them?'

'Practically all. The three or four absentees, one of them a girl, live a good way off, on farms, and weren't seen in the village that morning. Another, the butcher's son, has been in bed for nearly a month.

'Then we turned to a second possibility, that of mischief-making.

'Someone, any one of the neighbours, who'd quarrelled with old Leónie as nearly all of them had, someone she'd made fun of once too often, might, in a fit of anger, have fired from a distance, meaning to frighten her or break one of her windows, without even dreaming that she might be killed.

'I haven't quite rejected that theory yet, because the third possibility, that of deliberate murder, implies a crack shot, to begin with. If she'd been hit anywhere except in the eye, she'd have been only slightly wounded. And to shoot her deliberately in the eye from some distance, an exceptionally fine shot would be needed.

'Don't forget that this happened in broad daylight, in this group of buildings, at a time of day when most women are at home doing their housework. There's a maze of yards and gardens all around. It was a fine day, and most windows were open.'

'Have you tried to discover where everybody was at about a quarter past ten?'

'You heard Maria Smelker. The other statements aren't much clearer than hers. People are reluctant to answer questions. When they go into details they get so confused that it only complicates things.'

'The deputy-mayor was in his garden?'

'Apparently. It depends whether we're to go by wireless time or by the church clock, because the clock is fifteen or twenty minutes fast. Someone who was listening to the wireless claims to have seen Théo on his way to the *Bon Coin*, at about a quarter past ten. The people at the *Bon Coin* declare that he didn't arrive there till after half past ten. The butcher's wife, who was hanging out her washing, says she saw him go into his cellar for a drink, as he usually does.'

'Has he a rifle?'

'No. Only a double-barreled sporting gun. That shows you how difficult it is to get hold of reliable evidence. The boy's the only one whose statement holds together.'

'That's the policeman's boy?'

'Yes.'

'Why didn't he say anything the first day?'

'I asked him that. His reply is plausible. I expect you know that his father, Julien Sellier, is married to the old woman's niece?'

'Yes, and Léonie Birard had said she was disinheriting her.'

'Marcel Sellier felt it would look as though he were trying to shelter his father. He didn't mention it at home till the following evening. And Julien Sellier brought him along to us on Thursday morning. You'll be seeing them. They're pleasant people and seem to be sincere.'

'Marcel saw the schoolmaster coming out of his tool-shed?'

'So he says. The children were left to themselves in the classroom. Most of them were fooling around; Marcel Sellier, who's rather a serious, quiet boy, went across to the window and saw Joseph Gastin coming out of the shed.'

'He didn't see him go in?'

'Only coming out. The shot must have been fired then. The schoolmaster, however, stubbornly denies setting foot in the tool-shed that morning. Either he's lying, or the boy made up the story. But why?'

'Yes, why?' muttered Maigret in a detached tone.

He felt like a glass of wine. It was, he felt, the right time of day. The break was over, in the playground. Two old women went past with shopping-bags, on their way to the Co-operative.

'Might I have a look at Léonie Birard's house?' he asked.

'I'll take you there. I've got the key.'

That, too, was on the mantelpiece. He put it into his pocket, buttoned up his tunic and put his cap on. The air outside had a smell of the sea, but not enough to satisfy Maigret. They walked along to the corner of the street, and as they reached Louis Paumelle's inn, the chief-inspector asked casually:

'What about a drink?'

'Do you think so?' said the lieutenant, awkwardly.

He wasn't the type of man to go for drinks to a *bistrot* or an inn. The invitation embarrassed him, and he didn't know how to refuse.

'I wonder whether . . .'

'Just a quick glass of white wine.'

Théo was there, seated in a corner, his long legs outstretched, a jug of wine and a glass at his elbow. The postman, who had an iron hook where his left arm should have been, was standing in front of him. They both stopped talking as the other men came in.

'What will you take, gentlemen?' inquired Louis, who stood behind his bar, shirt-sleeves rolled up high.

'A *chopine*.'

Daniélou was uncomfortable, but trying to carry it off. Perhaps that was why the deputy-mayor stared mockingly at the two of them. He was tall and must once have been stout. Now that he had lost weight, his skin seemed to hang in folds, like a garment that was too loose.

The expression on his face combined the cunning self-assurance of the peasant with that of the politician, skilled in juggling with the village elections.

'Well, what's become of that scoundrel Gastin?' he inquired, as though speaking to nobody in particular.

And Maigret, without quite knowing why, retorted in the same tone:

'He's waiting for someone to go and take his place.'

The lieutenant was shocked at this. The postman turned his head sharply.

'You've discovered something?' he demanded.

'You must know the district better than anyone, you make the round of it every day.'

'And what a round! At one time, not so long ago, there were still people who practically never had any letters. I remember some farms where I only used to set foot once a year, to take the almanac. Nowadays they not only all get newspapers, which have to be delivered to them, but there isn't one who doesn't claim some allowance or pension. If you knew what a lot of papers that means! . . .'

He repeated, with an air of profound dejection: 'Papers! Papers!'

To hear him, one might have supposed that he had to fill them in himself.

'To begin with, there are the ex-servicemen. That I can understand. Then there are the widows' pensions. Then the health insurance, the large family allowances, and the allowances for . . .'

He turned to the deputy-mayor.

'Can you sort them all out? I sometimes wonder whether there's a soul in the village who doesn't draw something or other from the government. And I'm certain some of them have kids just for the sake of the children's allowance.'

His glass misted over in his hand, Maigret inquired jokingly:

'Do you think the allowances have something to do with Léonie Birard's death?'

'One never knows.'

It seemed to be an obsession. He must draw a pension himself, for his arm. He was paid by the government. And it infuriated him that other people benefited as well. In fact, he was jealous.

'Give me a *chopine*, Louis.'

Théo's eyes were still twinkling. Maigret drank his wine in sips, and this was almost like what he had expected of his trip to the seaside. The air was the same colour as the white wine, tasted the same. Out in the square, two hens were pecking at the hard ground; they could hardly be finding worms there. Thérèse was in the kitchen, peeling onions, wiping her eyes from time to time with the corner of her apron.

'Shall we be going?'

Daniélou, who had scarcely touched his wine, followed him with relief.

'Don't you think those peasants seemed to be laughing at us?' he murmured, when they were outside.

'And how!'

'You seem to find it funny!'

Maigret made no reply. He was beginning to find his feet in the village, and no longer regretted the Quai des Orfèvres. He hadn't telephoned to his wife that morning, as he had promised to do. He hadn't even noticed the post office. He'd have to take a look at that, presently.

They went past a haberdashery, and the chief-inspector saw, through the window, a woman so old and so emaciated that he felt she might snap in two at any moment.

'Who's that?'

'There are a couple of them, about the same age, the Demoiselles Thévenard.'

Two old maids had kept a shop in his native village, too. One would really think French villagers were interchangeable. Years had gone by. The roads had become crowded with fast cars. Buses and vans had replaced the former carts. Cinemas had sprung up all over the place. Wireless and numbers of other things had been invented. And yet Maigret was finding, in this village, the characters of his childhood, unchanged as figures in a holy picture.

'Here is the house.'

It was an old one, and the only one in the

street which had not been whitewashed for years. The lieutenant put the big key into the lock of the green-painted door, pushed it open, and they were met by a sickly smell, doubtless also to be found next door, where the two old maids lived, a smell that clings to places where very old people live with the windows shut.

The first room was not unlike the one where Madame Gastin had received him, except that the oak furniture was not so well polished, the upholstery was shabbier, and there was a set of huge copper fire-irons. There was also, in one corner, a bed which must have been brought in from another room, and which was still unmade.

'The bedrooms are upstairs,' explained the lieutenant. 'For the last few years Léonie Birard had refused to go up. She lived on the ground floor, slept in this room. Nothing has been touched.'

A half-open door led into a fair-sized kitchen, with a stone fireplace beside which a coal-burning kitchen range had been installed. Everything was dirty. Saucepans had left rusty circles on the stove. Splashes starred the walls. The leather arm-chair near the window must be the one in which the old woman had spent the greater part of her time.

Maigret understood why she preferred this room to the front one. There were hardly any passers-by on the road, which led to the sea, whereas from the back, just as from the schoolmaster's house, one could see the liveliest part of the houses, the yards and gardens, including the school playground.

It was almost homely. From her arm-chair, Léonie Birard could share the daily life of nine or ten families, and if she had sharp eyes she could see what they all had for their meals.

'The chalk line shows where she was found, of course. That stain you can see . . .'

'I understand.'

'She hadn't bled much.'

'Where is she now?'

'They took her to the morgue at La Rochelle, for the post-mortem. The funeral's tomorrow morning.'

'You still don't know who gets her property?'

'I've looked everywhere for a will. I telephoned to a solicitor at La Rochelle. She'd often talked to him about making a will, but she'd never done it with him. He has some securities she deposited with him, some bonds, the title-deeds of this house and of another one she owns, a mile from here.'

'So that if nothing is found, her niece will get the lot?'

'I imagine so.'

'What does she say about it?'

'She doesn't seem to count on it. The Selliers aren't hard up. They're not rich, but they have a flourishing little business. You'll be seeing them. I haven't your experience with people. These seemed frank, honest, hard-working.'

Maigret was opening and closing drawers,

discovering half-rusted kitchen utensils, odds and ends of all kinds, old buttons, nails, bills, jumbled up with threadless cotton-reels, stockings, hairpins.

He went back to the front room, where there stood an old chest of drawers which was not without value, and there too he opened the drawers.

'You've been through these papers?'

The lieutenant blushed slightly, as though he had been caught out or brought face to face with some disagreeable fact.

He had had the same expression at Louis's bar, when he had been obliged to take the glass of white wine held out to him by Maigret.

'They're letters.'

'So I see.'

'They go back more than ten years, to the time when she was still postmistress.'

'So far as I can see, they aren't addressed to her.'

'That's true. I shall put the whole lot in the file, of course. I've already mentioned them to the examining magistrate. I can't do everything at once.'

The letters were still in their envelopes, each of which bore a different name: Évariste Cornu, Augustin Cornu, Jules Marchandon, Célestin Marchandon, Théodore Coumar, and so on; women's names too, including those of the Thévenard sisters, who kept the haberdashery.

'It looks to me as though Léonie Birard, in the days when she was postmistress, didn't give *all* the letters to the people they were addressed to.'

He glanced over a few of them:

'Dear Mama,
    'This comes to tell you that I am well, as I hope you are. I like my new place, except that the grand-father, who lives with the family, coughs all day and spits on the floor. . . .'

Another said:

    'I met cousin Jules in the street and he looked ashamed when he saw me. He was dead drunk and for a moment I thought he didn't recognize me.'

Léonie Birard had evidently not opened all the letters. She seemed to be more interested in some families than in others—especially the Cornus and Rateaus, who were numerous in the district.

Several envelopes bore the Senate postmark. They were signed by a well-known politician who had now been dead for two years.

'My dear Sir,
    'I have received your letter about the storm that wrecked your mussel-beds and washed away more than two hundred posts. I am prepared to arrange for the funds earmarked for victims of national ca-lamities . . .'

'I asked about that,' explained the lieutenant. 'The mussel-beds consist of pinewood piles driven into the sea-bed, with bundles of twigs hung between them. The bunches of young mussels are slung there and left to grow. Whenever the tide comes in a bit violently, some of the piles are washed out to sea. They're expensive, because they have to be brought from a distance.'

'So the clever chaps get them paid for by the Government under the heading of "national calamity"!'

'That Senator was very popular,' said Daniélou with a wry smile. 'He never had any difficulty in getting re-elected.'

'You've read all these letters?'

'I've glanced through them.'

'They don't provide any clues?'

'They explain why the Birard woman was detested by everyone in the village. She knew too much about them all. She was probably pretty outspoken with them. But I found nothing really serious, anyhow nothing serious enough to induce anyone, especially after ten years had gone by, to finish her off with a bullet through the head. Most of the people those letters were meant for are dead now, and their children don't bother much about what went on in the old days.'

'Are you taking these letters away with you?'

'I needn't take them this evening. I can leave you the key of the house. You don't want to go upstairs?'

Maigret went up, to satisfy his conscience. He learnt nothing from the two upper rooms, which were full of odds and ends and pieces of dilapidated furniture.

Outside, he accepted the key the lieutenant proffered.

'What are you going to do now?'

'When is school over?'

'Morning class ends at half past eleven. Some of the children, those who live fairly near, go home for lunch. The rest, those who come from the farms and the seaside, bring sandwiches and eat them at school. Lessons begin again at half past one and finish at four o'clock.'

Maigret pulled out his watch. It was ten past eleven.

'Are you staying in the village?'

'I must go and see the examining magistrate, who's been questioning the schoolmaster this morning, but I'll be back sometime in the afternoon.'

'See you later, then.'

Maigret shook his hand. He felt inclined for another glass of white wine before the end of morning school. He stood for a moment in the sunshine, watching the lieutenant move away with a light step, as though a weight had fallen from his shoulders.

Théo was still at Louis's. In the opposite corner there now sat an old man dressed almost in rags, looking like a tramp, with a bushy white beard. Filling his glass with an unsteady hand, he had only an indifferent glance to spare for Maigret.

'A *chopine*?' inquired Louis.

'The same as before.'

'It's the only one I've got. I suppose you'll be

eating here? Thérèse is cooking a rabbit that'll make your mouth water.'

The maid appeared.

'You like rabbit with white wine sauce, Monsieur Maigret?'

It was only to get a glimpse of him, to shoot him a conspiratorial, grateful glance. He hadn't given her away. In her relief she looked almost pretty.

'You get along back to your kitchen.'

A van drew up, and a man in butcher's overalls came into the tap-room. Unlike most butchers he was thin and sickly-looking, with a crooked nose and bad teeth.

'A *pernod*, Louis.'

He turned towards Théo, who was smiling seraphically.

'Hello, you old scoundrel!'

The deputy-mayor's sole response was a vague movement of the hand.

'Not too tired? I can't think how lazy hounds like you get by!'

He switched his attention to Maigret.

'So it's you who're going to dig out the secret, is it?'

'I'm trying to!'

'Try hard. If you find anything you'll deserve a medal.'

He dipped his drooping moustache in his glass.

'How's your boy getting on?' asked Théo, still lazily sprawling in his corner.

'Doctor says it's time he began to walk. Easier said than done. As soon as he's put on his feet, he falls down. Doctors don't know their job. No more than deputy-mayors!'

He spoke jokingly, but with a bitter under-current in his voice.

'Have you finished your round?'

'I've still to go to Bourrages.'

He asked for a second glass, swallowed it at one gulp, wiped his moustache, and called to Louis:

'Chalk that up with the rest.'

Then, turning to the chief-inspector:

'Enjoy yourself!'

Finally, on his way out, he deliberately knocked against Théo's legs.

'So long, you dirty dog!'

They watched him start up the van and turn it in the square.

'His father and mother died of TB,' explained Louis. 'His sister is in a sanatorium. He's got a brother shut up in a lunatic asylum.'

'And he himself?'

'He does his best, sells his meat in the villages round here. He opened a butcher's shop at La Rochelle once, and it swallowed up every penny he'd got.'

'Has he several children?'

'A boy and a girl. The two others died at birth. The boy was knocked down by a motor-bike a month ago, and he's still in plaster. The girl, who's seven, is at school, I suppose. By the time he's finished his round he'll have swallowed at least half a bottle of *pernod*.'

'Amuses you, does it?' Théo asked in his mocking voice.

'What amuses me?'

'Telling all that.'

'I'm not saying any harm of anyone.'

'Would you like me to tell about your little affairs?'

This seemed to frighten Louis, who seized a *chopine* of wine from under the counter and went across to put it on the table.

'You know there's nothing to tell. One has to make conversation, doesn't one?'

Théo seemed somehow jubilant. His mouth was unsmiling, but there was a strange glint in his eyes. Maigret couldn't help thinking the man was like an old faun who'd retired from active life. There he was, in the midst of the village, like a mischievous god who knew everything that went on behind people's walls, inside people's heads, and who was watching with solitary relish the spectacle the world presented.

He regarded Maigret as an equal rather than an enemy.

'You're a very smart chap,' he seemed to be saying. 'You're supposed to be the star performer in your game. In Paris, you unearth everything people try to hide from you.

'But I'm a smart chap too. And down here, I'm the one who knows.

'Go ahead! Play your game. Ask people questions. Drag out their secret thoughts.

'We'll see whether you tumble to it in the end!'

He slept with Maria, an unlovely slattern. He had tried to sleep with Madame Gastin, who had nothing feminine left about her. He drank from morning to night, never entirely fuddled, floating in a private world which must be comic, since it brought a grin to his face.

The old woman Birard, too, had known the little village secrets, but they had infuriated her, acting on her like a poison that she had to work out of her system in one way or another.

His way was to watch the people, mock them, and when any of them wanted a fake certificate in order to draw one of those allowances that made the postman so angry, he supplied it, endorsing the paper with one of the *mairie* stamps which he always carried in the pockets of his shapeless trousers.

He didn't take them seriously.

'Another glass, Inspector?'

'Not just now.'

Maigret could hear children's voices from the direction of the school. Those who went home for lunch were coming out. He saw two or three going across the square.

'I'll be back in half an hour.'

'The rabbit will be ready.'

'Still no oysters?'

'No oysters.'

Hands in pockets, he strolled over to the Selliers' shop. A little boy had gone in just ahead of him, making his way among the buckets, hose-pipes, spraying apparatus that cluttered the floor and hung from the ceiling. There were other tools to be seen everywhere, in the dusty light.

A woman's voice asked:

'What can I do for you?'

He had to peer through the dimness to make out a youngish face, the light patch of a blue-and-white checked apron.

'Is your husband here?'

'At the back, in the workshop.'

The little boy had gone into the kitchen and was washing his hands at the pump.

'If you'll come this way, I'll call him.'

She knew who he was, and did not seem to be alarmed. In the kitchen, which was the centre of life in the house, she pushed forward a rush-bottomed chair for him, then opened a door into the yard.

'Julien! . . . Someone to see you. . . .'

The little boy was drying his hands and gazing inquisitively at Maigret. And he, too, brought childhood memories back to the chief-inspector. In his form at school, in every form he had been in, there had always been one boy who was fatter than the others and had this same inno-cent, intent expression, this same clear skin, this same air of having been well brought-up.

His mother was not a big woman, but his father, who came in a moment later, must have weighed well over fourteen stone; he was very tall, very broad, with an almost babyish face and guileless eyes.

He wiped his feet on the doormat before com-ing in. Three places were laid on the round table.

'Excuse me,' he murmured, going in his turn to the pump.

One could feel that in this house there was a ritual, each person doing certain things at certain times of day.

'Were you just going to have your meal?'

It was the woman who answered:

'Not at once. Dinner's not ready yet.'

'As a matter of fact, what I really wanted was to have a word with your little boy.'

Both parents looked at the child, with no sign of surprise or uneasiness.

'You hear that, Marcel?' asked his father.

'Yes, Papa.'

'Answer the inspector's questions.'

'Yes, Papa.'

Turning squarely to face Maigret, the boy settled into the attitude of a pupil preparing to answer his schoolmaster.

5

WHILE Maigret was lighting his pipe there took place a kind of silent ceremony which reminded him, more vividly than anything else he had seen at Saint-André since the previous evening, of the village of his childhood. For a moment, in fact, Madame Sellier seemed to have been transformed into one of his own aunts, in a blue-and-white checked apron, her hair screwed into a knot on top of her head.

The woman had merely looked at her husband, with the very slightest widening of her eyes, and Julien had understood the message, gone over to the back door, through which his tall figure had vanished for a moment. His wife, without waiting for him to come back, had opened the cupboard and taken out two glasses belonging to the best service, those that were kept for when visitors came, and she was now wiping them with a clean cloth.

When the ironmonger reappeared, he was carrying a corked-up bottle of wine. He said nothing. Nobody needed to say anything. Anyone who had come from a great distance, or from some other planet, might have imagined that these actions formed part of a rite. They heard the sound of the cork being drawn from the bottle, the splash of the golden wine into the two glasses.

Obviously a little shy, Julien Sellier picked up one glass, looked through it sideways, and finally said:

'Your very good health.'

'Your very good health,' responded Maigret.

After which the man withdrew to a shadowy corner of the room, while his wife went across to the stove.

'Tell me, Marcel,' began the chief-inspector, turning back to the boy, who had not moved, 'I suppose you've never told a lie?'

The hesitation, if any, was brief, accompanied by a quick sidelong glance towards his mother.

'Yes, sir, I have.'

He added hastily:

'But I've always confessed.'

'You mean you've gone to confession afterwards?'

'Yes, sir.'

'At once?'

'As soon as I could, because I didn't want to die in sin.'

'But they can't have been very important lies?'

'Pretty important.'

'Would you very much mind telling me one of them, as an example?'

'There was the time I tore my trousers, climbing a tree. When I got home I said I'd caught them on a nail in Joseph's yard.'

'And you went to confession that same day?'

'The next day.'

'And when did you own up to your father and mother?'

'Not till a week later. Another time I fell into the pond when I was catching frogs. Papa and Mamma don't let me play round the pond, because I catch cold easily. My clothes were all wet. I said another boy had pushed me when I was crossing the little bridge over the stream.'

'And did you wait a week that time, before telling them the truth?'

'Only two days.'

'Do you often tell lies like that?'

'No, sir.'

'About every how often?'

Marcel paused for reflection, just as though this were an oral examination.

'Less than once a month.'

'Do your friends do it more often?'

'Not all of them. Some do.'

'Do they go to confession afterwards, like you?'

'I don't know. I expect so.'

'Is the schoolmaster's son a friend of yours?'

'No, sir.'

'Don't you play with him?'

'He doesn't play with anybody.'

'Why not?'

'Perhaps because he doesn't like playing. Or perhaps because his father's the teacher. I did try to be friends with him.'

'You don't like Monsieur Gastin?'

'He's unfair.'

'In what way unfair?'

'He always gives me top marks, even when it's his son who ought to have them. I like to be top of the class when I've deserved it, but not when I haven't.'

'Why do you suppose he does that?'

'I don't know. Perhaps he's afraid.'

'Afraid of what?'

The boy struggled to find a reply. He undoubtedly knew what he wanted to say, but realized that it was too complicated, that he wouldn't find the words. He merely repeated:

'I don't know.'

'You remember Tuesday morning?'

'Yes, sir.'

'What did you do during break?'

'I played with the others.'

'What happened a little time after you'd gone back to the classroom?'

'Old Piedbœuf, from Gros-Chêne, knocked on the door, and Monsieur Gastin went over to the *mairie* with him, after telling us to keep quiet.'

'Does that often happen?'

'Yes, sir. Fairly often.'

'Do you keep quiet?'

'Not all of us.'

'You yourself keep quiet?'

'Most of the time.'

'When had this happened last?'

'The day before, on Monday, when there was a funeral. Someone came to have a paper signed.'

'What did you do on Tuesday?'

'At first I stayed in my place.'

'Had the other boys begun to fool about?'

'Yes, sir. Most of them.'

'What exactly were they doing?'

'They were fighting for fun, throwing things at each other, india-rubbers and pencils.'

'And then?'

The boy occasionally hesitated before replying, but not from embarrassment, merely like someone searching for the exact answer.

'I went to the window.'

'Which window?'

'The one overlooking the yards and kitchen gardens. That's the one I always go to.'

'Why?'

'I don't know. It's the one nearest to my desk.'

'It wasn't the sound of a shot that made you go to the window?'

'No, sir.'

'If a shot had been fired outside, would you have heard it?'

'I mightn't have. The others were making a lot of noise. And a horse was being shod at the forge.'

'Have you a .22 gun?'

'Yes, sir. I took it to the *mairie* yesterday, like the others. Everybody who had a gun was asked to take it to the *mairie*.'

'You didn't leave the classroom while the master was away?'

'No, sir.'

Maigret was speaking in a quiet, encouraging tone. Madame Sellier had tactfully departed to tidy the shop, while her husband, glass in hand, was watching Marcel with an air of pride.

'You saw the schoolmaster crossing the yard?'

'Yes, sir.'

'You saw him when he was on his way to the tool-shed?'

'No, sir. He was coming back from it.'

'You saw him come out of the shed?'

'I saw him shutting the door behind him. Then he came across the yard and I said to the others:
' "Look out!"

'Then they all went back to their places. Me too.'

'Do you play a great deal with the other boys?'

'Not much, no.'

'Don't you like playing?'

'I'm too fat.'

He blushed as he said this, glanced at his father, as though apologizing.

'Haven't you any friends?'

'Joseph's my best friend.'

'Who's Joseph?'

'Monsieur Rateau's son.'

'The mayor's son?'

Julien Sellier broke in to explain.

'There are a lot of Rateaus at Saint-André and in the neighbourhood,' he said, 'nearly all cousins. Joseph's father is Marcellin Rateau, the butcher.'

Maigret took a sip of wine and relit his pipe, which he had allowed to go out.

'Was Joseph with you at the window?'

'He wasn't at school. He's been at home for a month, because of his accident.'

'Is he the boy who was knocked down by a motor-bicycle?'

'Yes, sir.'

'Were you with him when it happened?'

'Yes, sir.'

'Do you often go to see him?'

'Nearly every day.'

'Did you go yesterday?'

'No.'

'The day before yesterday?'

'Not then either.'

'Why not?'

'Because of what had happened. Nobody was thinking of anything except the crime.'

'You wouldn't have dared to tell a lie to the constabulary lieutenant, I suppose?'

'No, sir.'

'Are you glad the schoolmaster's in prison?'

'No, sir.'

'Do you realize it's your evidence that sent him there?'

'I don't understand what you mean.'

'If you hadn't said you'd seen him coming out of the tool-shed, they probably wouldn't have arrested him.'

He made no reply to this, embarrassed, shifting from one foot to the other, glancing again at his father.

'If you really did see him, you were quite right to tell the truth.'

'I did tell the truth.'

'You didn't like Léonie Birard?'

'No, sir.'

'Why not?'

'Because she used to shout rude things at me when I went past.'

'More at you than at the others?'

'Yes, sir.'

'Do you know why?'

'Because she was cross with Mamma for marrying my father.'

Maigret half closed his eyes, trying to think of another question, failed to find one and emptied his glass instead. He rose to his feet, rather heavily, for he had already that morning drunk quite a few glasses of white wine.

'Thank you, Marcel. If you had anything to say to me—for instance, if you remembered any little thing you'd forgotten, I'd like you to come and see me at once. You're not scared of me?'

'No, sir.'

'Another glass?' asked the boy's father, reaching out for the bottle.

'No, thank you. I don't want to delay your

lunch any longer. Your son's an intelligent boy, Monsieur Sellier.'

The ironmonger flushed with pleasure.

'We're doing our best to bring him up properly. I don't think he often tells lies.'

'That reminds me: when did he tell you about the schoolmaster going to the tool-shed?'

'On Wednesday evening.'

'He hadn't said anything about it on Tuesday, when the whole village was talking about Léonie Birard's death?'

'No. I think he was a bit overcome. On Wednesday, while we were at dinner, he looked rather strange, and suddenly he said to me:

' "Papa, I think I saw something."

'He told me the story, and I went and reported it to the police lieutenant.'

'Thank you.'

Something was bothering him, he didn't know exactly what. Once outside, he made first for the *Bon Coin*, where he saw the substitute schoolmaster seated near the window, eating his lunch and reading a book. He remembered he had meant to telephone to his wife, walked to the post office, which was one of another group of houses, and was received there by a girl of about twenty-five, who wore a black overall.

'Would it take very long to get Paris?'

'Not at this time of day, Monsieur Maigret.'

While he waited for his call he watched her doing her accounts, wondered whether she was married, whether she would get married one day, or if she would turn out like the old Birard woman.

He stayed in the telephone booth for about five minutes, and the only words the girl at the switchboard could hear through the door were:

'No, no oysters. . . . Because there aren't any. . . . No. . . . The weather's lovely. . . . Not in the least cold. . . .'

He decided to go to lunch. The schoolmaster was still there, and Maigret was shown to a seat at the opposite table. The whole village knew who he was by this time. They didn't speak to him, but they watched him go along the street, and no sooner had he gone by, than they began to talk about him. The schoolmaster looked up from his book three or four times. Just as he went away he seemed to hesitate for a moment. Perhaps he had something he wanted to say? One couldn't be sure. In any case, as he went past he gave him a nod which might have been interpreted as an unintentional jerk of the head.

Thérèse had a spotless white apron over her black dress. Louis was eating in the kitchen, where he could be heard calling to the girl from time to time. When he had finished he came over to Maigret, his mouth still greasy.

'Well, what did you think of the rabbit?'

'It was first-class!'

'A drop of *marc* to wash it down? This is on me.'

His manner towards the chief-inspector was protective, as though without him he would have been lost in the jungle of Saint-André.

'Queer chap, that!' he growled as he sat down, legs wide apart because of his fat stomach.

'Who?'

'Théo. Cleverest fellow I know. All his life he's managed to take things easy, without doing a stroke of work.'

'Do you really think nobody else heard that shot?'

'Well, in the country, people don't pay much attention to a rifleshot. If it had been a sporting gun, everybody would have noticed. But those little things don't make much noise, and we've got so used to them since all the kids began to have them. . . .'

'Théo was in his garden and is supposed not to have seen anything?'

'In his garden or in his wine-cellar, since what he calls gardening usually means going to tap the barrel. But if he did see anything he probably wouldn't say so.'

'Even if he saw someone fire the shot?'

'All the more reason to keep quiet.'

Louis was pleased with himself, refilled the little glasses.

'I warned you you wouldn't understand a thing.'

'Do you believe the schoolmaster wanted to kill the old woman?'

'Do you?'

Maigret replied positively:

'No.'

Louis looked at him, smiling as though to say: 'Neither do I.'

But he did not say it. The two of them were probably in the same torpid condition, because of what they had had to eat and drink. They sat in silence for a moment, looking out at the square which was cut in two by the sun, at the greenish glass windows of the co-operative stores, the stone porch of the church.

'What's the priest like?' asked Maigret, for the sake of something to say.

'He's a priest.'

'Is he on the schoolmaster's side?'

'No.'

At last Maigret got up, stood hesitating for a moment in the middle of the room, then decided on laziness and moved towards the staircase.

'You can call me in an hour,' he said to Thérèse.

He had been wrong to use the familiar 'tu'. Officials at Police Headquarters usually speak like that to women of her type, and it had not been lost on Louis, who frowned. In the bedroom the green shutters were closed, with only thin shafts of sunlight stealing through. He did not undress, only took off his jacket and shoes, lay on the bed without turning it down.

A little later, while he was still only dozing, he seemed to hear the regular sound of the sea—could it be that? Then he went right off to sleep and did not wake until there was a knock on the door.

'It's more than an hour, Monsieur Maigret. Would you like a cup of coffee?'

He still felt heavy, sluggish, uncertain as to what he really wanted to do. Downstairs, going

through the front room, he saw four men playing cards; one was Théo and another Marcellin,
the butcher, still in his working clothes.

He still felt there was a detail jarring somewhere, though he couldn't think what it was.
He had had that impression during his talk with
little Sellier. At what moment exactly?

He began walking, first to Léonie Birard's
house, the key of which was in his pocket. He
went in, sat down in the front room, where he
read all the letters he had glanced over that
morning. They did not tell him anything important, merely familiarized him with certain
names, the Dubards, the Cornus, the Gillets,
Rateaus and Boncœurs.

On leaving the house he meant to go down
the path to the sea, but a little way along he
found the cemetery and went in, spelt out the
names on the tombs, much the same as those
he had found in the letters.

He could have pieced together the family his-
tories, telling how the Rateaus had been related
by marriage to the Dubards for two generations
back, and that a Cornu daughter had married a
Piedbœuf who had died at the age of twenty-
six.

He went on for another two or three hundred
yards, and the sea was still not in sight, the
meadows were sloping gently upwards on either side; all he could see, far ahead, was a shimmering mist that he gave up hope of reaching.

The villagers kept meeting him in their streets
and alleys, hands in pockets, stopping now and

then, aimlessly, to stare at a house-front or a passer-by.

He couldn't resist another glass of white wine before going to the *mairie*. The four men were still playing cards and Louis sat astride a chair, watching the game.

The sun was shining full on the *mairie* steps, and looking down the corridor he could see the caps of the two *gendarmes*, in the kitchen garden at the back. They must be still hunting for the cartridge-case.

The windows of the schoolmaster's house were shut. Rows of children's heads could be seen through the schoolroom window.

He found the lieutenant making notes, in red pencil, on a witness's statement.

'Come in, Chief-Inspector. I've seen the examining magistrate. He questioned Gastin this morning.'

'How is he?'

'Like a man who's just spent his first night in prison. He was anxious to know whether you were still here.'

'He sticks to his denial, I suppose?'

'Closer than ever.'

'Has he any theory of his own?'

'He doesn't believe anyone meant to kill the old woman. He thinks it was more likely a practical joke that proved fatal. People often played tricks of that kind.'

'On Léonie Birard?'

'Yes. Not only the children, but grown-ups as

well. You know what it is when a whole village takes a dislike to someone. Whenever a cat died it would be tossed into her garden, if it wasn't thrown through the window into the house. A couple of weeks ago she found her door all plastered with dung. The schoolmaster thinks someone fired a shot to frighten her or make her angry.'

'What about the tool-shed?'

'He still makes out that he never set foot in it on Tuesday.'

'He didn't do any gardening on Tuesday morning, before school?'

'Not on Tuesday, but on Monday he did. He gets up at six o'clock every morning, it's only then that he has a little time to himself. Did you see the Sellier boy? What do you think about him?'

'He answered my questions without hesitation.'

'Mine, too, without once contradicting himself. I questioned the other boys, who all declare he didn't leave the classroom after break. If that had been a lie, I imagine one of them would certainly have slipped up on it.'

'I imagine so. Do they know who inherits?'

'They still haven't found a will. Madame Sellier's chances look good.'

'Did you check on how her husband spent his time on Tuesday morning?'

'He was busy in his workshop.'

'Any witnesses to that?'

'His wife, for one. And for another, Marchandon, the blacksmith, who went across to speak to him.'

'What time was that?'

'He doesn't know exactly. Before eleven o'clock, he says. According to him, they chatted for at least a quarter of an hour. Not that that proves anything, of course.'

He leafed through his papers.

'Especially as young Sellier says the forge was working when the schoolmaster left the classroom.'

'So his father could have gone away?'

'Yes, but don't forget that everybody knows him. He'd have had to go across the square and into the gardens. If he'd been carrying a rifle they'd have noticed him all the more.'

'But they mightn't say so.'

In fact there was nothing reliable, no firm foundation, except two contradictory statements: one from Marcel Sellier, who said that from the schoolroom window he had seen Gastin coming out of the tool-shed; and the other from Gastin himself, who would swear that he had never set foot in the shed that day.

All these happenings were recent. The villagers had been questioned on the evening of the very day, Tuesday, and the questioning had gone on during Wednesday. They had had no time to forget things.

If the schoolmaster had not fired the shot, why should he tell a lie? And, above all, what motive had he for killing Léonie Birard?

Neither had Marcel Sellier any motive for making up the tool-shed story.

As for Théo, he maintained, in his bantering style, that he had heard a shot, but seen nothing at all.

Had he been in his kitchen garden? Had he been in his wine-cellar? Impossible to rely on the times given by any of them, for time doesn't count much in the country, except when it comes to meals. Neither was Maigret very convinced by assurances that such and such a person had or had not gone past along the street at a particular moment. When you're accustomed to seeing people a dozen times a day in the same familiar places, you don't pay attention any longer, and you may quite sincerely mix up one meeting with another, say that a particular incident took place on Tuesday whereas really it happened on Monday.

The wine was making him feel hot.

'What time is the funeral?'

'Nine o'clock. Everybody will be there. It isn't every day that they have the pleasure of burying the local bugbear. Have you got an idea?'

Maigret shook his head, went on pottering about the office, fingered the rifles, the lead pellets.

'I believe you told me the doctor wasn't certain what time she was killed?'

'He puts it at between ten and eleven in the morning.'

'So that if it weren't for young Sellier's evidence . . .'

They always came up against that. And each time, Maigret had the same impression that the truth had given him the slip again, that he had been on the verge, at one moment, of discovering it.

He wasn't interested in Léonie Birard. What did it matter to him whether someone had meant to kill her or only to frighten her, or whether it was by accident that the bullet had gone through her left eye?

It was the Gastin business that excited him, and consequently, little Sellier's evidence.

He walked into the courtyard, and was halfway across it when the children began emerging from the schoolhouse, less hurriedly than at break, and making their way in small groups to the gate. Brothers and sisters could be distinguished among them. The big girls were leading smaller children by the hand, and some of them would have nearly two miles to walk home.

Only one boy greeted him, except Marcel Sellier, who raised his cap politely. The others went past, staring inquisitively. The schoolmaster was standing in the doorway. Maigret went up to him and the young man stepped aside to let him in, stammering:

'Did you want to speak to me?'

'Not particularly. Had you been to Saint-André before this?'

'No. This is the first time. I've taught in schools at La Rochelle and at Fourras.'

'Did you know Joseph Gastin?'

'No.'

The desks and forms were black, cut about with penknives and splashed with patches of purple ink, which had a bronze sheen here and there against the varnish. Maigret went to the first window on the left, through which he saw part of the courtyard, the gardens, the tool-shed. Then, from the right-hand window, he could see the back of Léonie Birard's house.

'Did you notice anything special about the children's behaviour today?'

'They're quieter than town children. Perhaps they're shy.'

'They've not been holding discussions in groups, or passing notes in class?'

The deputy teacher was less than twenty-two years old. He was obviously in awe of Maigret, rather because he was a celebrity than because he belonged to the police. He would no doubt have behaved in the same way if confronted with a famous politician or a film star.

'I'm afraid I didn't pay attention to that. Should I have done?'

'What do you think of young Sellier?'

'Just a moment . . . which one is that? . . . I don't know their names yet. . . .'

'A taller, fatter boy than the others, who's very good at his lessons. . . .'

The young man's eyes turned towards the seat at the end of the front row, which was evidently Marcel's place, and Maigret went and sat down there, though the desk was too low for him to get his knees under it. Sitting here and looking out of the second window, it was not the kitchen gardens he saw, but the lime-tree in the court-yard and the Gastins' house.

'He didn't strike you as uneasy or worried?'

'No. I remember asking him some questions in arithmetic and noticing that he was very intelligent.'

To the right of the schoolmaster's house, further off, one could see the first-floor windows of two other houses.

'Tomorrow I may perhaps ask you to let me come and see them for a moment during school.'

'Whenever you like. We're both staying at the inn, I believe. It'll be easier for me to prepare my lessons over here.'

Maigret left him, and was about to go to the schoolmaster's house. It was not Madame Gastin he wanted to see, but Jean-Paul. He walked more than half the distance, saw a curtain move at one of the windows, stopped, depressed at the thought of finding himself once again in a stuffy little room, confronted with the tragic faces of the woman and her little boy.

He felt cowardly. Overcome by laziness which must be due to the leisurely village life, the white wine, the sun which was now beginning to sink behind the roofs.

What, in fact, was he doing here? Scores of times before, during an investigation, he had had this same feeling of helplessness, or rather of futility. He was suddenly pitchforked into the life of a group of people he had never set eyes on before, and his job was to worm out their deepest secrets. This time it wasn't even his job.

He had come of his own accord, because a schoolmaster had waited for him for hours in the Purgatory at Police Headquarters.

The air was taking on a bluish tint, becoming cooler, damper. Windows were lighting up here and there, and Marchandon's forge stood out, red; one could see the flames dancing every time the bellows blew them.

In the shop opposite were two women, as motionless as the picture on an advertisement calendar, with only their lips moving slightly. They seemed to be speaking in turns, and at the end of every sentence the shopwoman shook her head disconsolately. Were they talking about Léonie Birard? Very likely. And about tomorrow's funeral, which would be a memorable event in the history of Saint-André.

The men were still playing cards. They must spend hours this way, every afternoon, exchanging the same phrases, now and again putting out a hand to pick up a glass, then wipe their lips.

He was about to go in, order a *chopine* for himself, sit down in a corner to wait for dinnertime, when a car pulled up close beside him, making him jump.

'Did I frighten you?' called the cheery voice of the doctor. 'You haven't fathomed the mystery yet?'

He got out of the car, lit a cigarette.

'Makes a change from the Grands Boulevards,' he remarked, with a wave of the hand at the village around them, the dimly-lit shop-windows, the forge, the church door, which was half open, letting out a faint glow of light. 'You should just see it in the middle of the winter. Have you begun to get used to our local life?'

'Léonie Birard used to keep letters addressed to different people.'

'She was an old scoundrel. Some people called her the louse. You can't imagine how scared she was of dying!'

'Was she ill?'

'Ill enough to have died long ago. But she didn't die. Like Théo, who ought to have been in his grave these ten years or more, and yet goes on drinking his two quarts of white wine a day, not to mention *apéritifs*.'

'What do you think of the Selliers?'

'They're doing their best to join the middle class. Julien came here as an apprentice from the Waifs and Strays, and worked hard to establish himself. They've only one child, a boy.'

'I know. He's intelligent.'

'Yes.'

It seemed to Maigret that there was a certain reserve in the doctor's tone.

'What do you mean?'

'Nothing. He's a well-brought-up lad. He's one of the choirboys. The priest's pet.'

It looked as though the doctor didn't like priests, either.

'You believe he's been lying?'

'I didn't say that. I don't believe anything. If you'd been a country doctor for twenty-two years, you'd be like me. The only thing that interests them is making money, turning it into gold, putting the gold into bottles and burying the bottles in their gardens. Even when they're ill or injured, they have to make something out of it.'

'I don't understand.'

'There's always the insurance, or the allowances, one way or another of turning everything into money.'

He was talking almost like the postman.

'A bunch of scoundrels!' he concluded, in a tone which seemed to contradict his words. 'They're a scream. I'm quite fond of them.'

'Léonie Birard too?'

'She was phenomenal!'

'And Germaine Gastin?'

'She'll spend the rest of her life tormenting herself and everybody else because she went to bed with Chevassou. I'll bet it didn't happen often, perhaps only once. And just because she enjoyed herself once in her life . . . If you're still here tomorrow, come and have lunch with me. This evening I have to go to La Rochelle.'

It was dark already. Maigret hung about a little longer in the square, emptied his pipe, knocking the bowl against his heel, and, with a sigh, went into Louis's inn, walked over to a table which was already his table, and Thérèse, without being asked, put a *chopine* of white wine and a glass in front of him.

Théo, sitting opposite with his pack of cards, glanced at him from time to time with eyes that sparkled with malice, as though to say:

'You're coming on: You're coming on: A few years of that, and you'll be like the rest of them.'

6

I T was not because of the postmistress's funeral, which was to take place that day, that Maigret woke up with a weight on his mind. The death of Léonie Birard, in the sunshine, had not upset anyone, there had been nothing tragic about it, and the people of Saint-André, in the houses and farms, were doubtless dressing for her burial as cheerfully as for a wedding. So much so that Louis Paumelle, out in the yard very early, already wearing his starched white shirt and black cloth trousers, but with no collar or tie, was pouring wine into an impressive number of *chopines*, which he was lining up not only behind the bar, but on the kitchen table as well, as though this were a fair-day.

The men were shaving themselves. Everybody would be wearing black, as though the whole village were in mourning. Maigret remembered how once, when he was little, his father had asked one of his aunts why she had bought yet another black dress.

'Well you know, my sister-in-law has cancer of the breast and may be dead in a few months or even in a few weeks. It is so bad for clothes, to dye them!'

In any village people have so many relations who may die any moment, that they spend all their time dressed in black.

Maigret shaved himself, too.

He saw the La Rochelle bus go off almost empty, although this was a Saturday. Thérèse had brought him up a cup of coffee and his hot water, because she had seen him sitting for hours in his corner, the previous evening, drinking wine and then, after dinner, glass upon glass of brandy.

But it wasn't, either, because of the amount he had drunk, that he now had a feeling of tragedy. Perhaps, after all, it was simply because he had slept badly. All night he had been seeing children's faces, in close-up, as though at the cinema, faces which all resembled little Gastin and little Sellier, but were not exactly either of theirs.

He tried, without success, to recall those dreams. Someone had a grudge against him, one of the boys; he couldn't say which, they were indistinguishable. He kept telling himself that it was easy to recognize them apart, because the schoolmaster's son wore glasses. But immediately afterwards he saw Marcel Sellier wearing glasses too and saying, when he expressed surprise:

'I only put them on when I go to confession.'

Gastin's being in prison was not so very tragic, for the police lieutenant did not really believe he was guilty; neither, in all probability, did the examining magistrate. He was better off there for a few days than going about the village or shut up in his own house. And he couldn't be found guilty on the evidence of a single witness, especially when that witness was a child.

It seemed to Maigret to be more complicated than that. This often happened to him. One could even say that during each case that came along, his mood followed more or less the same curve.

At the beginning you see people from the outside. Their little traits are what show most clearly, and that's amusing. Then, gradually, you begin to put yourself in their shoes, to wonder why they behave in this or that fashion; you catch yourself thinking like them, and that's much less amusing.

Later on, perhaps, when you've seen so much of them that nothing surprises you any longer, you may be able to laugh at them, like Dr. Bresselles.

Maigret had not reached that stage. He was worried about the little boys. At least one of them, somewhere, he felt must be living in a kind of nightmare, in spite of the bright sunlight that was still shining over the village.

By the time he went downstairs to his corner

for breakfast, farmers from the outlying districts were already arriving in the square in carts. They did not come straight into the café, but stood in dark-clad groups in the street and outside the church, and their tanned skin made their shirts look dazzling white by contrast.

He did not know who had made the arrangements for the funeral, it had not occurred to him to ask. In any case the coffin had been brought from La Rochelle and taken straight to the church.

The black figures were rapidly increasing in number. Maigret noticed faces he had not seen before. The police lieutenant came up and shook hands.

'Anything fresh?'

'Not a thing. I saw him last night in his cell. He sticks to his denial, can't understand why Marcel Sellier persists in accusing him.'

Maigret went into the school playground; there were to be no lessons today, and the windows of the schoolmaster's house were closed, no one to be seen: the boy and his mother would certainly not go to the funeral, they would stay at home, silent, terrified, waiting for something to happen.

But the crowd did not seem to be angry. The men were calling to one another, some were going into Louis's for a quick glass, and coming out again, wiping their lips. As the chief-inspector went past they all fell silent, then began to talk in low voices, following him with their eyes.

A young man who, despite the cloudless sky, was wearing a tightly-belted raincoat, came up to him, an outsized pipe in his mouth.

'Albert Raymond, reporter on *La Charente*,' he announced cockily. He was not more than twenty-two. He was thin, long-haired, kept his mouth twisted into a sardonic smile.

Maigret merely nodded.

'I tried to get along to see you yesterday, but I hadn't the time.'

His way of speaking and general manner implied that he felt himself to be on equal terms with the chief-inspector. Or rather, that they were both outside this crowd. They could both look down on it with condescension, as men who knew, who had penetrated to the most hidden springs of human nature.

'Is it true,' he asked, grasping his pencil and notebook, 'that the schoolmaster came and offered you all his savings if you'd get him out of the mess?'

Maigret turned towards him, looked him up and down, was about to say something, then, with a shrug of the shoulders, turned his back on him.

The idiot would probably think he'd guessed right. It didn't matter. The bells were ringing. The women were pouring into the church, with a few men as well. Then came the soft notes of the organ, the tinkle of a choirboy's bell.

'Is it to be a mass, or only an intercession?' the chief-inspector inquired of a man he did not know.

'A mass and an intercession. We've got plenty of time.'

Time to go to Louis's for a drink. Most of the men had gradually gathered in front of the inn or went inside in groups to drink a *chopine* or two of wine without sitting down, and then emerge again. There was a perpetual coming and going: there were people in the kitchen and even in the yard. Louis Paumelle, who had already been into the church for a moment, was now in his shirt-sleeves again and bustling about, helped by Thérèse and by a young man who seemed to be accustomed to lending him a hand.

Sellier was in church, with his wife. Maigret had not seen Marcel go past, but a little later, when he too went to the church, he understood why. Marcel was there, in his choirboy's surplice, serving mass. He could apparently get straight into the vestry by going through his parents' backyard.

'*Dies irae, dies illa . . .*'

The women really seemed to be praying, their lips were moving. Were they praying for Léonie Birard's soul, or for themselves? A few old men were standing, hat in hand, at the back of the nave, and others peeped in from time to time, half opening the door, to see how the service was getting along.

Maigret went out again, caught sight of Théo, who acknowledged his presence with his usual juicy, sarcastic grin.

Somebody obviously must know. There might even be several who knew and were keeping quiet. The voices in Louis's bar-parlour were growing louder now, and one thin farmer, with a drooping moustache, was already more than half drunk.

The butcher, too, seemed to Maigret to have brighter eyes and a more unsteady gait than usual, and the chief-inspector saw him drain three large glasses within a few minutes, invited by one man or another.

The lieutenant, either less inquisitive than he or more sensitive to the curiosity of the crowd, had taken refuge in the office at the *mairie*, where the courtyard was empty around its lime-tree.

A cart went by, which was to serve as a hearse, drawn by a chestnut horse with a black rug draped over its back. It pulled up outside the porch and the driver came across for a drink.

A light breeze was stirring the air. Far up in the sky, a few clouds were gleaming like mother-of-pearl.

At length the church doors opened. The drinkers rushed outside. The coffin appeared, carried by four men among whom Maigret recognized Julien Sellier and the deputy-mayor.

It was hoisted, not without difficulty, on to the cart. It was then covered with a black, silver-fringed pall. Young Sellier appeared next, bearing a silver cross on a black wooden shaft, and his surplice blew out round him two or three times, like a balloon.

The priest followed, repeating prayers, finding the time to glance at each person in turn; his eyes lingered for a moment on Maigret's face.

Julien Sellier and his wife led the procession; both were in black and she had a veil over her face. Next came the mayor, a tall, powerful man with a placid face and grey hair, surrounded by the members of the local council, then the general public, men in front and women behind; some of the latter, especially those at the tail end of the procession, were dragging children by the hand.

The young journalist was hurrying to and fro, making notes, talking to people whom Maigret did not know. Slowly the procession moved on, passing Louis's inn where Thérèse stood alone in the doorway, for Paumelle was with the local councillors' group.

For the second time that morning, Maigret was tempted to go and knock on the Gastins' front door and talk to Jean-Paul. Now that all the inhabitants were off to the cemetery, the mother and son must surely be feeling lonelier than ever in the deserted village.

He followed the others, however, for no definite reason. They went past Léonie Birard's house, then past a farm; a calf in the farmyard began to bellow.

As they turned into the cemetery there was a certain amount of trampling and confusion. The priest and the choirboy were already at the graveside before the rest had all come through the gate.

It was then that Maigret noticed someone looking over the wall. He recognized Jean-Paul. One of his glasses was reflecting the sun like a mirror.

Instead of following the crowd, the chief-inspector remained outside and began to walk round the cemetery, meaning to join the boy. The latter was, he thought, probably too concentrated on what was happening beside the grave to notice this manœuvre.

He was walking along a strip of waste ground. He had got to within about thirty yards of the boy, when he trod on a dead branch.

Jean-Paul looked round quickly, jumped down from the stone he had been standing on, and bolted for the road.

Maigret was about to call to him, refrained because the others would have heard him, merely walked on more quickly, hoping to catch up with the boy on the road.

The situation was, he realized, ridiculous. He could not venture to run. Neither could Jean-Paul. The child was afraid even to glance behind him. He was probably the only one in the village who was wearing his school clothes, not dressed in his best.

To make his way home, as he probably wanted to do, he would have had to pass the cemetery gate, outside which stood a group of farmers.

He turned left, towards the sea, hoping, perhaps, that the chief-inspector would not follow him.

Maigret followed. There were no more farms or houses to be seen, only fields and meadows where a few cows were grazing. The sea was still invisible, behind a low hill. The road sloped gently upwards.

The boy was walking as fast as he could do without breaking into a run, and Maigret, too, had lengthened his stride. He did not even know exactly why he was pursuing him like this, began to realize it was cruel.

To Jean-Paul it must seem as though a terrifying power were on his tracks. But the chief-inspector could not very well begin to shout:

'Jean-Paul! . . . Stop! . . . I only want to talk to you. . . .'

The cemetery had vanished behind them, and the village. Little Gastin had now reached the top of the hill and began to go down the other side; and Maigret could only see his head and shoulders, then only his head. There came a moment when he saw nothing at all, until he, in his turn, reached the top of the hill; and then, at last, the sparkling expanse of sea lay before him, with what he took to be an island in the distance, or perhaps the Pointe de l'Aiguillon, and a few brown-sailed fishing-boats, looking as though they were floating in space.

Jean-Paul was still walking. There was no path, either to right or left. Down beside the sea stood five or six red-roofed huts, where the mussel-breeders kept their tackle.

'Jean-Paul!' he made up his mind and called.

His voice sounded so strange that he hardly recognized it, and he turned his head to make sure nobody was watching. He noticed a momentary change in the rhythm of the boy's step. Surprise at hearing his name called had made him hesitate, almost pause, but now the surprise was over he was walking as fast as ever, practically running, panic-stricken.

The chief-inspector was ashamed of his persistence, he felt like a hulking brute bearing down on a defenceless creature.

'Wait for me, boy. . . .'

What made the position even sillier was that he was out of breath and his voice didn't carry. The distance between them remained about the same. To reduce it, he would have had to run.

What was Jean-Paul hoping? That Maigret would be disheartened and turn back?

It was more likely that he wasn't thinking at all, that he was just plunging on as though it were the only hope of escaping a danger. All that lay ahead of him was the sea, its shining fringe of foam washing over the pebbles.

'Jean-Paul . . .'

At the point he had reached, it would be as silly to give up as to go on.

The boy came to the beach, halted as though uncertain whether to take the path which no doubt led to the next village, finally stopped, still with his back turned, and only when he heard the chief-inspector's footsteps quite close by, did he swing round to face him.

He was not red but pale, his nostrils pinched. His chest was visibly heaving fast, his lips were parted, it seemed as though his heart-beats must be audible, like those of a bird held in the hand.

Maigret said nothing. For the moment he could think of nothing to say, and he, too, was out of breath.

126

Jean-Paul had turned away from him and was looking at the sea. They both stared in that direction, and the silence lasted a long time, as long as was needed for their hearts to return to a calm, regular rhythm.

Then Maigret walked a few steps and sat down on a stack of posts which smelt of fresh pinewood. He took off his hat, unashamedly mopped his forehead, and began, very slowly, to fill his pipe.

'You're a fast walker,' he muttered at last.

The boy, who was standing with his legs braced like a young cock, made no reply.

'Won't you come and sit by me?'

'I don't want to sit down.'

'Are you angry?'

Jean-Paul threw him a quick glance and asked: 'Why?'

'I wanted to talk to you without your mother being present. At your home it can't be done. When I saw you over the cemetery wall, I thought that was my chance.'

So as not to startle the child, he paused for a long time between sentences.

'What were you looking at?'

'The people.'

'You couldn't have been watching them all at the same time. I'm sure you were watching one particular person. Am I right?'

Jean-Paul neither admitted this nor denied it.

'Do you usually go to church?'

'No.'

'Why not?'

'Because my father and mother don't go.'

Conversation would have been easier with a grown-up. It was so long since Maigret's childhood. He had no son or daughter of his own. But he had to try to see things from this boy's standpoint.

'Did you tell your mother you were going out this morning?'

'No.'

'You didn't want her to know?'

'She'd have stopped me.'

'So you waited till she was upstairs, so as to slip out quietly? And you went round by the back lanes?'

'I wanted to see.'

'What?'

It wasn't the crowd, nor the coffin being lowered into the grave. Maigret felt certain of that.

He remembered the surplice puffed out by the wind, and the cross Marcel had been carrying; he recalled the time when, hardly seven years old, he himself had yearned to be a choirboy. He had had to wait two years. Then it had been his turn to carry the silver cross and trot towards the cemetery, with a rustic hearse following behind.

'You wanted to see Marcel?'

He saw the boy give a start, the astonishment of the child on suddenly realizing that a grown-up is capable of guessing his thoughts.

'Why aren't you friends with Marcel?'

'I'm not friends with anyone.'

'Is there no one you like?'

'I'm the schoolmaster's son, I told you that already.'

'You'd rather be the ironmonger's son, or the mayor's, or the son of one of the local farmers?'

'I didn't say that.'

It was important not to frighten him, for he would have been capable of taking to his heels again. Yet it was not only fear of being caught up by Maigret that kept him where he was. He could move faster than the chief-inspector. Could it be that now they were face to face he felt a kind of relief? Could it be that at the bottom of his heart he had a secret longing to talk to somebody?

'Won't you sit down now?'

'I'd rather stand.'

'Are you very sorry your father's in prison?'

Instead of replying at once in the negative, he said nothing.

'You aren't sorry?'

Maigret was feeling like a stalker, creeping forward only with infinite caution. He must not go too quickly. The slightest word would be enough to startle the child, and then there would be nothing to be got out of him.

'Does it make you unhappy to be different from the others?'

'Why am I different from the others? Who said I was?'

'Suppose I had a little boy and he went to school, and played in the street near our home. The other boys would say,

' "His father's the chief-inspector!"

'And because of that, they wouldn't treat him quite like one of themselves. You understand?

'Well, your father is the schoolmaster.'

The little boy looked at him again, longer and more intently than before.

'Would you have liked to be in the choir?'

He could feel he was on the wrong track. It was hard to say how he knew it. Some of the things he had said caused an almost imperceptible reaction. Others seemed to make Jean-Paul close up in himself.

'Marcel has friends?'

'Yes.'

'When they're together, they talk in whispers? They tell one another secrets, begin to laugh when they look at the rest of you?'

This was all coming back to him from so long ago that it astonished him. Never before, he thought, had he recalled such vivid memories of his own childhood; he could even smell the scent of the lilacs that flowered in the school playground in spring-time.

'Have you tried to be friends with them?'

'No.'

'Why not?'

'No reason.'

'You thought they wouldn't want you?'

'Why are you asking me all these questions?'

'Because your father's in prison. He didn't shoot Léonie Birard.'

He was staring hard at the boy, who did not blink.

'You know quite well he didn't. So someone else must have done it. Would you like your father to be found guilty?'

'No.'

There had been an almost imperceptible hesitation, and Maigret decided to let this point drop. It had occurred to him already, sitting in his corner the evening before, that Jean-Paul might feel some concealed resentment against his father and mother for being different from other people.

Not only because his father was the schoolmaster. They didn't go to church. They didn't dress him the same way as the other boys. Their house wasn't like the other houses either, nor was their way of life. His mother never laughed, she glided about like a shadow, humble and contrite. She had done something very wrong, and a woman had shot at her, to punish her.

The woman hadn't been sent to prison, which proved that she must have been right.

But perhaps Jean-Paul was fond of them all the same. Whether he liked it or not, he belonged to their clan, their race.

It was difficult to express all this. There were shades of meaning that vanished when one tried to put them into words.

'Suppose you knew something that would get your father out of prison . . .'

He himself didn't know what he was making for, and was surprised when Jean-Paul suddenly raised his head, stared at him with a mixture of terror and admiration. The boy opened his mouth, was about to say something, but bit it back, clenching his fists in the effort to restrain himself.

'Look, I'm only trying to understand. I don't

know your father very well, but I feel sure he's not a man to tell lies. He says he didn't set foot in the tool-shed on Tuesday morning, and I believe him.'

The boy, still on the defensive, continued to watch him closely.

'On the other hand, Marcel Sellier seems like a good boy. When he does tell a lie, he goes to confession at once, so as not to remain in a state of sin. He has no reason to make trouble for your father. He's never unfair to him, in fact always puts him at the top of the class when you're the one who should be there.

'But Marcel says he saw your father coming out of the shed.'

It was like a bubble bursting suddenly at the surface of a pool. Jean-Paul, hanging his head, without looking at Maigret, declared:

'He's telling a lie.'

'You're quite sure of that, aren't you? It isn't just your own impression. You aren't saying it out of jealousy.'

'I'm not jealous of Marcel.'

'Why didn't you say so before?'

'What?'

'That Marcel was telling a lie.'

'Because!'

'You're quite certain he didn't see your father?'

'Yes.'

'What makes you so certain?'

Maigret had expected tears, perhaps even screams, but Jean-Paul's eyes, behind his spectacles, were dry. Only, his body had relaxed. There was nothing aggressive in his attitude now. He was not even on the defensive any longer.

The only visible sign of his surrender was that, feeling unsteady on his feet, he now sat down, at a little distance from the chief-inspector.

'I saw him.'

'Who did you see?'

'Marcel.'

'Where? When?'

'In class, standing by the window.'

'Tell me exactly what happened.'

'Nothing happened. Monsieur Piedbœuf came to fetch Father. They went together to the *mairie* office.'

'You saw them go?'

'Yes. I could see them from where I sat. They went in at the front door, and all the other boys began to fool about, as usual.'

'You stayed at your desk?'

'Yes.'

'Don't you ever fool about?'

'No.'

'Where was Marcel?'

'Standing by the first window on the left, the one that looks on to the playground and the gardens.'

'What was he doing?'

'Nothing. He was just looking out.'

'Doesn't he fool around either?'

'Not often.'

'Sometimes?'

'When Joseph's there.'

'The butcher's son?'

'Yes.'

'You were sitting at your desk. Marcel was standing at the left-hand window. Your father and Monsieur Piedbœuf were in the office. That's right, is it?'

'Yes.'

'Were the windows open?'

'They were shut.'

'You could hear the noise of the forge all the same?'

'I think so. I'm almost certain.'

'What happened?'

'Marcel left the window and walked across the room.'

'Where was he going?'

'To one of the two windows on the right.'

'The one that overlooks the back of Madame Birard's house?'

'Yes.'

'Your father was still at the *mairie* then?'

'Yes.'

'Marcel didn't say anything?'

'No. He looked out of the window.'

'You don't know what he was looking at?'

'From where I was sitting I couldn't see.'

'Do you often watch Marcel?'

He admitted awkwardly:

'Yes.'

This time, Maigret did not ask him why. The two boys were both good at their lessons, but because Jean-Paul was the schoolmaster's son, Marcel was put at the head of the class. Marcel was a choirboy and wore a surplice on Sundays.

Marcel had friends, he had Joseph, the butcher's son, with whom he talked in whispers at break and to whose house he went to play when school was over.

'You saw your father come out of the *mairie* after that?'

'He walked over to our house, and went in for a cup of coffee.'

'Was the kitchen window open?'

'No. I know he had a cup of coffee. He always does.'

'Was your mother downstairs?'

'Upstairs in my room. I could see her through the open window.'

'After that your father didn't go into the tool-shed?'

'No. He came across the playground, back to the classroom.'

'Marcel was still standing at the window, the one on the right?'

'Yes.'

'Why didn't you say so at once?'

'When?'

Maigret paused for a moment to sort out his recollections.

'Wait a minute. Léonie Birard's body was found at the beginning of the afternoon. They didn't question you children at once?'

'They didn't question us at all that day. We didn't know exactly what had happened. We just noticed people coming and going. Then we saw the *gendarmes*.'

In fact, on Tuesday no one had openly accused

the schoolmaster. Marcel Sellier had said nothing, either to his parents or to anyone else. So Jean-Paul had had no reason to contradict him and no chance of doing so.

'Were you there next day, when they questioned Marcel?'

'No. They sent for us one by one, in the office.'

'And when he came back on Thursday morning? When did you first hear that he was maintaining he had seen your father?'

'I can't remember now.'

'Did your parents talk about Léonie Birard on Tuesday evening?'

'Not till I was in bed. I heard part of what they were saying. Mother said it was her fault. Father said no, it was only rumors, people would soon realize he'd had nothing to do with it.'

'Why didn't you protest when you discovered that Marcel was accusing him?'

'Nobody would have believed me.'

Again Maigret seemed to catch a flicker, a mere nothing, something too subtle to be put into words. The little boy had not been pleased when his father was accused. He had probably been rather ashamed to think that he was in prison. But hadn't he been rather cowardly? Hadn't he been tempted, however slightly, without admitting it even to himself, to desert his parents' cause?

He already bore them a grudge for not being like other people. Now they were even less like other people, and the village, instead of simply cold-shouldering them, had turned against them.

Jean-Paul envied Marcel.

Was he to accuse him in his turn?

When one came to think of it, he had not been carried away by bad feelings. It hadn't been a question of cowardice, at any rate not only of cowardice.

Couldn't it even be said to be a kind of loyalty to the others?

He had had a chance of contradicting Marcel, showing him up as a liar. It would have been easy. Had it seemed to him to be too easy, too cheap a triumph?

Besides, it was a fact that people wouldn't have believed him. Who indeed in the village would have believed him, if he had gone to them and said:

'Sellier is a liar. My father didn't come out of the tool-shed. I saw him go into our house, come out again, cross the playground. And at that time Marcel was standing at the opposite window, where he couldn't see him.'

'You haven't told this to your mother?'

'No.'

'Is she crying a lot?'

'She doesn't cry.'

That was even worse. Maigret could imagine the atmosphere in their house during the last few days.

'Why did you come out this morning?'

'To see.'

'To see Marcel?'

'Perhaps.'

Perhaps also, without realizing it, from an urge to share, even at a distance, in the village life? He must surely feel smothered in that little house at the far end of the yard, where his mother was afraid to open the windows.

'Are you going to tell the lieutenant?'

'I must have a word with Marcel first.'

'Will you tell him you heard about it from me?'

'Would you rather he didn't know that?'

'Yes.'

It looked as though he hadn't entirely given up hope of one day being admitted to the alluring company of Marcel, Joseph and the rest.

'I think he'll tell me the truth without my needing to bring you into it. Some of the others must have seen which window he was standing by.'

'They were fooling about.'

'All of them?'

'All except one of the girls, Louise Boncœur.'

'How old is she?'

'Fifteen.'

'Doesn't she fool about with the rest of them?'

'No.'

'You think she was watching Marcel?'

For the first time the boy's face was red, especially his ears.

'She watches him all the time,' he mumbled.

Was it because she was in love with Marcel that she hadn't contradicted him, or simply because she hadn't distinguished between one window and another? Marcel had said he was standing by the window. The other children probably hadn't thought twice about which one it had been.

'It's time we went back to the village.'

'I'd rather not go back with you.'

'Would you like to go ahead?'

'Yes. You're sure you won't say anything to Marcel?'

Maigret nodded, and the boy hesitated, touched his cap, set out in the direction of the fields, soon breaking from a walk into a run.

The chief-inspector, who was at last by the sea, forgot to look at it, was gazing after the small figure departing along the lane.

Then he set out in his turn, stopped to fill his pipe, blew his nose, muttered something unintelligible, and anyone seeing him advancing slowly along the road would doubtless have wondered why he shook his head every now and then.

When he went past the cemetery the gravediggers had finished heaping yellowish earth on Léonie Birard's coffin; her tomb could be recognized from a long way off, because of the bunches of flowers and fresh wreaths.

7

THE women had gone home and, except for a few who came from distant farms, had probably taken off their black dresses and best shoes by this time. The men were still there, as though this were fair-day, and were overflowing from Louis's inn on to the pavement and into the yard, where they stood, putting down their bottles on the windowsills or on an old iron table that had been left outside all winter.

The pitch of their voices, their laughter, their slow, fuddled gestures made it clear that they had drunk a lot, and one, whose face Maigret did not see, was relieving himself behind the hedge.

Thérèse, busy as she was, had found time to pass him a *chopine* and a glass. He had gone only a few paces into the room, and could hear snatches of several conversations at once; he had

had a glimpse of the doctor in the kitchen, but there were so many people in the way that he could not join him for the moment.

'I'd never have thought we'd have had the burying of her,' one old man was saying, shaking his head.

There were three of them, all much of an age. All three were certainly over seventy-five, and behind them, as they stood in a corner, against the white wall, was a copy of the law on establishments for the sale of alcoholic beverages and on public intoxication. They held themselves more stiffly than usual, because of their black Sunday suits and starched shirts, and this lent them a certain solemnity.

It was strange to see that though their faces were wrinkled with deep furrows, their eyes, when they looked at one another, had an innocent, childish expression. Each of them had a glass in his hand. The tallest of the three, who had a magnificent crop of white hair and a silky moustache, was swaying slightly, and whenever he was disposed to speak he laid a finger on the shoulder of one of his companions.

Why did Maigret suddenly imagine them in the school playground? They were just like schoolboys in their laughter and in the glances they exchanged. They had been to school together. Later in life they had pulled the same girls into ditches and had seen one another married, attended the funerals of their respective parents, their children's weddings and the christenings of their grandchildren.

'She might almost have been my sister; my father used to tell me he didn't know how often he'd pushed her mother down under the haystack. It seems she was a hot bitch and her husband was a cuckold from start to finish.'

Didn't that go far to explain the village? Behind Maigret, in another group, someone was saying:

'When he sold me that cow, I said to him:

' "Look here, Victor, I know you're a thief. But don't forget we did our military service together at Montpellier, and there was that evening . . ." '

Louis hadn't had time to change, he had only taken off his jacket. Maigret was edging slowly forward, remembering that the doctor had invited him to lunch at his house that day. Could Bresselles have forgotten about it?

He had a glass in his hand, like everyone else, but he had not lost his head, and was trying to quieten Marcellin, the butcher, who was the most drunk of them all and seemed very excited. It was difficult, from a distance, to make out exactly what was going on. Marcellin appeared to be angry with somebody, was trying to thrust the little doctor aside and push his way into the front room.

'I tell you I'm going to tell him!' the chief-inspector heard him say.

'Be quiet, Marcellin. You're drunk.'

'I've a right to be drunk, haven't I?'

'What did I tell you the last time you came to me for a check-up?'

'Be damned to what you told me!'

'If you go on like this, the next funeral will be yours.'

'I won't be spied on. I'm a free man.'

Wine did not suit him. He was white-faced, with an unhealthy flush on his cheekbones and eyelids. He was losing control of his movements. His voice was becoming thick.

'You hear that, Doc? I never could stand spies. And what's he doing here, except . . .'

It was Maigret he was looking at, from a distance, struggling to rush at him and vent his feelings. Two or three of the others were watching him and laughing. Someone held out a glass, which the doctor intercepted, emptying its contents on the ground.

'Don't you see he's had a skinful, Firmin?'

So far there had been no quarrelling, no scuffle. Indeed, they all knew one another too well to start fighting, and everyone knew exactly who was strongest among them.

Maigret went no closer; to avoid irritating the butcher he pretended not to notice what was going on. But he kept an eye on the group, and witnessed a little scene which distinctly surprised him.

The tall figure of Théo, the deputy-mayor, came lounging up, with the usual glint of mockery in his eyes, and joined the others; he was brandishing a glass which contained not wine but *pernod*, a strong dose, to judge by the colour.

He made some remark to the doctor in an undertone and passed the glass to the butcher, laying a hand on his shoulder. He said something to him too, and Marcellin at first seemed inclined to struggle, to push him away.

Finally, he grabbed the glass, swallowed its contents at one gulp, and almost at once his eyes glazed over, losing all expression. He made one more attempt to point a threatening finger at the chief-inspector, but his arm had grown too heavy to lift.

Whereupon, as though he had just felled him with a blow, Théo pushed him towards and up the stairs; after the first few steps he had to hoist him on to his shoulder.

'You haven't forgotten my invitation?'

The doctor, who had walked across to Maigret, gave a sigh of relief as he remarked, in almost the same words as the old man in the corner:

'*They've put her underground*! Shall we go now?'

They both slipped through the crowd and out on to the pavement, where they strolled a few steps.

'Before three months are up it'll be Marcellin's turn. I'm telling him regularly:

' "Marcellin, if you don't stop drinking you won't last long!"'

'He's reached a stage where he eats practically nothing.'

'He's a sick man?'

'They're all sick, in his family. He's a pathetic case.'

'Théo's putting him to bed upstairs?'

'He had to be got rid of somehow.'

He opened the door. There was a good smell of cooking in the house.

'Will you have an *apéritif*?'

'Thank you, I'd rather not.'

The smell of wine had been so strong at Louis's inn that one could have got drunk just by breathing it in.

'Did you see the funeral?'

'From a distance.'

'I looked for you as I left the cemetery, but I didn't see you. Is lunch ready, Armande?'

'In five minutes.'

Only two places were laid. The doctor's sister, just like a priest's housekeeper, preferred not to sit down at table. She no doubt took her meals standing up in the kitchen, between two courses.

'Sit down. What do you think about it?'

'About what?'

'About nothing. About everything. She had a terrific funeral!'

Maigret grunted: 'The schoolmaster's still in prison.'

'Somebody had to go there.'

'I'd like to ask you a question, Doctor. Do you think that among all that crowd at the funeral there were many people who believed that Gastin killed Léonie Birard?'

'There must have been a few. Some people will believe anything.'

'And what about the rest?'

At first the doctor did not see the point of the question. Maigret explained:

'Let's suppose that one person in ten believes that Gastin fired that shot.'

'That's about the proportion.'

'Then the other nine-tenths have their own idea.'

'Undoubtedly.'

'Who do they suspect?'

'That depends. In my opinion each of them suspects, more or less sincerely, the person he himself would prefer to be found guilty.'

'And nobody says anything about it?'

'Among themselves, I expect they do.'

'Have you heard any such suspicions expressed?'

The doctor looked at him with something of Théo's irony.

'They don't say that kind of thing to me.'

'But although they know or believe that the schoolmaster is innocent, it doesn't worry them that he's in prison.'

'It assuredly doesn't worry them. Gastin isn't a local man. They consider that if the constabulary lieutenant and the examining magistrate have thought fit to arrest him, that's their affair. That's what those two are paid for.'

'Would they let him be condemned?'

'Without batting an eyelid. Of course, if it had been one of their own folk, it'd be a different story. Are you beginning to understand? If there has to be a guilty party, they'd rather it was an outsider.'

'Do they think the Sellier boy is telling the truth?'

146

'Marcel's a good boy.'

'He's told a lie.'

'Perhaps so.'

'I wonder why.'

'He may have thought his father would be accused. Don't forget that his mother is old Léonie's niece and will get all she's left.'

'I thought the old post-woman had always said her niece wouldn't get a penny.'

The doctor looked slightly embarrassed. His sister brought in the *hors-d'œuvre*.

'Did you go to the funeral?' Maigret asked her.

'Armande never goes to funerals.'

They began to eat in silence. Maigret was the first to break it, by saying, as though to himself:

'It wasn't on Tuesday that Marcel Sellier saw Gastin coming out of the tool-shed, it was on Monday.'

'He's admitted that?'

'I haven't asked him yet, but I'm practically certain of it. On Monday, before school, Gastin worked in his garden. Going across the playground during the morning, he noticed a hoe lying around and went to put it away. On Tuesday evening, after the body had been found, Marcel said nothing, and it didn't occur to him to accuse his teacher then.

'The idea came to him later, or some conversation he overheard made him decide to do it.

'He didn't tell an outright lie. Women and children specialize in such half-lies. He didn't make anything up, he simply changed a real event to another day.'

147

'That's rather comic!'

'I'll bet he's trying now to convince himself that it really was on Tuesday that he saw the schoolteacher coming out of the shed. He can't manage it, of course, and he must have been to confession.'

'Why don't you ask the priest?'

'Because if he told me, he'd be indirectly betraying the secrets of the confessional. The priest won't do that. I was thinking of asking the neighbours, the people at the co-operative stores, for instance, whether they'd seen Marcel going into the church at a time when there was no service, but now I know he goes in from the courtyard.'

The mutton was done to a turn and the beans melted in the mouth. The doctor had produced a bottle of old wine. A dull humming sound could be heard from outside, the noise of people talking in the inn yard and on the square.

Did the doctor realize that Maigret was simply talking in order to try out his ideas on a listener? He was going round and round the same subject, lazily, never coming right to the point.

'Actually, I don't think it was to save his father from suspicion that Marcel told that lie.'

At that moment he had the impression that Bresselles knew more about the matter than he would admit.

'Really?'

'You see, I'm trying to look at things from a child's point of view. From the very beginning I've had the impression that this is some children's business in which grown-ups have become mixed up just by accident.'

Looking the doctor straight in the face he added placidly, weightily:

'And I'm more and more convinced that other people know it too.'

'In that case perhaps you'll be able to persuade them to talk?'

'Perhaps. It's difficult, isn't it?'

'Very difficult.'

Bresselles was laughing at him, just as the deputy-mayor did, again.

'I had a long talk with the little Gastin boy this morning.'

'You went to their house?'

'No. I saw him watching the funeral, over the cemetery wall, and I followed him down to the sea-shore.'

'Why did he go down to the sea?'

'He was running away from me. At the same time he wanted me to catch up with him.'

'What did he tell you?'

'That Marcel Sellier was standing at the right-hand window, not the left. Marcel might, at a pinch, have seen Léonie Birard fall when the bullet hit her in the eye, but he couldn't possibly have seen the schoolmaster coming out of the shed.'

'What conclusion do you draw from that?'

'That it was in order to protect somebody that little Sellier decided to tell his lie. Not at once. He took his time. The idea probably didn't enter his head straight away.'

'Why did he choose the schoolmaster?'

'For one thing because he was the most likely person. And for another because it just so happened that he'd seen him the day before, almost at the same time, coming out of the shed. And perhaps because of Jean-Paul, too.'

'You think he hates him?'

'I'm not saying anything positive, Doctor. I'm simply groping in the dark. I've questioned both boys. This morning I was watching some old men who were children themselves once, in this very village. If the village people are so liable to be hostile to strangers, isn't it because, without realizing it, they're envious of them? They themselves spend the whole of their lives at Saint-André, except for a trip to La Rochelle now and then, with only an occasional wedding or funeral by way of distraction.'

'I see what you're getting at.'

'The schoolmaster comes from Paris. In their eyes, he's an educated man who pokes into their little affairs and takes upon himself to give them advice. Among the children, the schoolmaster's boy has much the same status.'

'So Marcel told his lie because he hates Jean-Paul?'

'Partly because he envies him. The funny thing is that Jean-Paul, on his side, envies Marcel and his friends. He feels lonely, different from the others, rejected by them.'

'All the same, somebody shot the old Birard woman, and it can't have been either of the boys.'

'That's true.'

A home-made apple-tart was brought in, and the smell of coffee came in from the kitchen.

'I feel more and more convinced that Théo knows the truth.'

'Because he was in his garden?'

'Because of that and for other reasons. Last night, Doctor, you informed me cheerfully that they were all scoundrels.'

'I was joking.'

'Only half-joking, isn't that it? They all cheat, to some extent, they all go in for what you would call little mean tricks. You're an outspoken man. You haul them over the coals now and then. But you'd never actually give them away. Or am I wrong?'

'You say the *curé* would refuse to answer any questions you might put to him about Marcel, and I think you're right. Well, I'm their doctor. It's the same thing, in a way. Doesn't it strike you, Inspector, that this lunch is beginning to be rather like an interrogation? What will you have with your coffee? Brandy or *calvados*?'

'*Calvados.*'

Bresselles got up to fetch the bottle from an antique sideboard, and filled the glasses, still gay and playful, but his eyes rather more serious now.

'Your good health.'

'I'd like to talk to you about the accident,' said Maigret, almost timidly.

'What accident?'

It was only to gain time for thought that the doctor asked this question, for accidents in the village were few and far between.

'The motor-bicycle accident.'

'You've heard about that?'

'All I've heard is that Marcellin's son was knocked down by a motor-bike. When did it happen?'

'One Saturday, just over a month ago.'

'Near old mother Birard's house?'

'Not far away. A hundred yards, perhaps.'

'In the evening?'

'Not long before dinner-time. It was dark. The two boys . . .'

'What boys?'

'Joseph, Marcellin's lad, and Marcel.'

'Were they by themselves?'

'Yes. They were going home. A motor-bike came up from the direction of the beach. Nobody knows exactly how it happened.'

'Who was on the bike?'

'Hervé Jusseau, a man of about thirty, who owns some mussel-beds, and got married last year.'

'Was he drunk?'

'He doesn't drink. He was brought up by his aunts, who are very strict and who still live in his house.'

'Was his headlamp lit?'

'Yes, that was established by the inquiry. The boys must have been playing about. Joseph tried to cross the road, and got knocked down.'

'Was his leg broken?'

'In two places.'

'Will he be lame?'

'No. In a week or two he'll be as good as new.'

'He can't walk yet?'

'No.'

'Will Marcellin get anything out of the accident?'

'The insurance will pay a fair amount, because Jusseau admitted that it was probably his fault.'

'Do you think it was?'

The doctor was obviously ill at ease, and took refuge in a burst of laughter.

'I'm beginning to understand what you chaps at Police Headquarters mean by "third degree" questioning. I'd rather come clean. That's what you call it, isn't it?'

He refilled the glasses.

'Marcellin's a pathetic chap. Everyone knows he won't last much longer. He can't be blamed for drinking, because he's been unlucky all his life. There's always been illness somewhere in his family, and everything he's undertaken has gone wrong. Three years ago he rented some pasture-land to fatten bullocks, and there was such a drought that he lost every penny. He can hardly make both ends meet. His van is more often broken down by the roadside than on its way delivering meat.'

'So Jusseau, who, being insured, has nothing to lose, took the blame on himself?'

'That's about it.'

'Everyone knows this?'

'Pretty well everyone. An insurance company

is a vague, far-away set-up, like the government, and people feel quite justified in taking money off it.'

'You made out the certificates?'

'Of course.'

'And worded them in such a way that Marcellin would get the highest possible sum?'

'Let's say I stressed the possibility of complications.'

'Were there any complications?'

'There might have been. As often as not, when a cow dies of some sudden illness, the vet certifies that it was an accident.'

It was Maigret's turn to laugh.

'Unless I'm mistaken, Marcellin's boy might have been up and about for the last week or two.'

'For the last week.'

'By keeping the plaster on his leg, you're enabling his father to demand more money from the insurance?'

'Even the doctor has to be a bit of a scoundrel, you see. If I refused that kind of thing, I'd have been gone from here long ago. And it's because the schoolmaster won't oblige with certificates, that he's in prison today. If he'd been more adaptable, if he hadn't been constantly scolding Théo for being too generous with Government money, they might have ended by adopting him.'

'In spite of what happened to his wife?'

'All the men here are cuckolds themselves.'

'So Marcel Sellier was the only witness of the accident?'

'I told you it was after dark. There was nobody else on the road.'

'Somebody might have seen them from a window.'

'You're thinking of old Léonie?'

'Well, I suppose she wasn't *always* in her kitchen; she must have gone into the front room now and then.'

'There was no mention of her during the inquiry. She didn't come forward.'

The doctor scratched his head, perfectly serious now.

'I have the impression you're beginning to see your way. Not that I can follow you yet.'

'Are you sure of that?'

'Of what?'

'Why did Marcellin try to throw himself on me this morning?'

'He was drunk.'

'Why pick on me particularly?'

'You were the only stranger in the inn. When he's tight he gets persecution mania. So he began to imagine you'd come here simply to spy on him. . . .'

'You were trying hard to calm him down.'

'Would you have preferred a fight?'

'Théo finished him off by making him drink a double or triple *pernod*, and carted him upstairs. It's the first time I've seen the deputy-mayor do a good turn.'

'Marcellin's his cousin.'

'I'd rather he'd been allowed to come out with what he wanted to say to me.'

The others had obviously wanted to stop him talking, they'd whisked him away, so to speak, and at present he must be sleeping off his drink in one of the first-floor bedrooms.

'I must be getting back to my surgery,' said Bresselles. 'There'll be at least a dozen people in the waiting-room by now.'

The consulting surgery was a low-roofed, two-roomed building in the yard. People could be seen sitting in a row against the wall; among them a child with a bandaged head and an old man with crutches.

'I think you'll end by getting somewhere!' sighed the little doctor, referring, of course, not to Maigret's career, but to the present investigation.

His attitude now betokened some respect, but a certain embarrassment as well.

'You'd rather I didn't find out anything at all?'

'I'm wondering. It might have been better if you hadn't come.'

'That depends on how it's all going to end. Have you no idea about that?'

'I know about as much as you do on the subject.'

'And you'd have left Gastin in prison?'

'They can't keep him there for long, in any case.'

Bresselles wasn't a local man. He was a townsman like the schoolmaster. But he had been living with the village for over twenty years, and couldn't help feeling himself a part of it.

'Come and see me whenever you like. Please

believe I do what I can. It's just that I'd rather live here and spend most of my day on the road, than be shut up in a surgery in a town or in some suburb or other.'

'Thank you for the lunch.'

'Are you going to question young Marcel again?'

'I haven't decided yet.'

'If you want him to talk, you'd better see him when his father isn't there.'

'Is he afraid of his father?'

'I don't think it's that. It's more that he admires him. If he's told a lie he must be in a state of terror.'

When Maigret emerged from the house, there were only a few people clustered at Louis's and on the square. Théo was sitting in a corner, playing cards, as on any other day, with the postman, the blacksmith and a farmer. His eyes met Maigret's, and though they were still mocking they held a dawning respect as well.

'Is Marcellin still upstairs?' the chief-inspector asked Thérèse.

'Snoring! He's messed up the whole room. He can't carry drink any longer. The same thing happens every time.'

'Nobody been asking for me?'

'The lieutenant came past just now. He didn't come in, he only gave a glance round as though looking for somebody, it may have been you. Will you have something to drink?'

'No, thank you.'

The very smell of wine was making him feel

sick. He strolled over to the *mairie*. One of the gendarmes was talking to Lieutenant Daniélou.

'Were you wanting to see me?'

'Not specially. I went across the square a little time ago and took a look in case you were at the inn.'

'Nothing fresh?'

'It may be of no importance. Nouli, here, has found a seventh rifle.'

'A .22?'

'Yes. Here it is. It's the same type as the others.'

'Where was it?'

'In the stable behind the butcher's house.'

'Hidden?'

It was the gendarme himself who replied:

'I was still hunting for the cartridge-case, with one of the other men. We were going through the gardens. I noticed that one of the stable doors was open, and there were bloodstains all over the place. Then I saw the rifle in a corner.'

'Did you question the butcher's wife?'

'Yes. She said that when Sellier went round with his drum to announce that all rifles must be taken to the *mairie*, she forgot all about her little boy's gun, because he was in bed. He had an accident about a month ago, and . . .'

'I know.'

Maigret stood holding the weapon, puffing at his pipe. Finally he put down the rifle, propping it in a different corner from the others.

'Will you come with me for a moment, Lieutenant?'

They went across the courtyard and opened the door of the schoolroom, which smelt of ink and chalk.

'Now I don't know yet where this is going to lead us. On Tuesday morning, when the school-master left this room with Piedbœuf, the farmer, Marcel Sellier came over to this window.'

'That's what he told us.'

'To the right of that lime-tree, one can see the tool-shed. One can also see certain windows, including those on the first floor of the butcher's house.'

The lieutenant was listening, with a slight frown.

'The boy didn't remain here long. Before the schoolmaster left the office, he went to the other side of the classroom.'

Maigret was doing the same, walking past the blackboard and the teacher's desk to the window right opposite the first one.

'From here, as you can see for yourself, there's a view of Léonie Birard's house. If, as the in-vestigation seems to have established, she was standing at her window when she was shot, Marcel may have seen her fall.'

'You think he had some reason for crossing from one window to the other? He might have seen something, and . . .'

'Not necessarily.'

'Why did he tell a lie?'

Maigret preferred not to answer this.

'You have suspicions?'

'I think so.'

'What are you going to do?'

'What has to be done,' replied Maigret without enthusiasm.

He sighed, emptied his pipe on the greyish floorboards, looked down at the ashes with an air of embarrassment and added, as though regretfully:

'It isn't going to be pleasant.'

From a first-floor window in the opposite house, Jean-Paul was watching them across the courtyard.

8

BEFORE he left the classroom, Maigret noticed another figure, at a window, an open one this time, in a more distant house, beyond the gardens. Someone was sitting on the windowsill, with his back turned, but from the shape of the head and the plump body, he recognized Marcel Sellier.

'That's the butcher's house, I suppose?'

The lieutenant followed the direction of his glance.

'Yes . . . Joseph, the son, and Marcel are great friends.'

The boy at the window turned round and looked down at a woman who was hanging out washing in a garden. Automatically, his eyes swept round in a half-circle just as Maigret and the lieutenant were coming out of the school and facing his way.

In spite of the distance it was clear, from his movements, that he was saying something to somebody in the room; then he slid off the windowsill and disappeared.

Daniélou turned to the chief-inspector and said quietly, pensively:

'Good luck!'

'Are you going back to La Rochelle?'

'Would you rather I waited for you?'

'If you did I might perhaps be able to take the evening train.'

He had not more than a hundred and fifty yards to go. He covered the distance at a swinging stride. The butcher's was a low, squat house. There was no proper shop. The left-hand ground-floor room had been fitted up for the purpose with a quaint-looking counter, a pair of scales, an old-fashioned refrigerator and a table on which the meat was cut up.

The front door opened into a passage at the far end of which, to the left of the stairs, one saw through to the backyard.

Before knocking, Maigret had gone past the right-hand window, the kitchen window, which was open; inside, at a round table, sat three women, one of whom was old and wore a white cap; they were eating slices of tart. One of them must be Marcellin's wife and the others her mother and sister, who lived in the neighbouring village and had come over for the funeral.

They had seen him go by. The windows were so small that for a moment his bulk had blocked this one. They listened while he paused at the open door, looked for a bell and, not finding one, took two steps forward, purposely making a noise.

The butcher's wife got up, half-opened the kitchen door, began by asking:

'What is it?'

Then, recognizing him, probably from having seen him about the village, she went on:

'You're the policeman from Paris, aren't you?'

If she had been to the funeral, she had already changed her clothes. She could not be very old, but she was round-shouldered, hollow-cheeked, with feverish eyes. Avoiding his eye, she added:

'My husband's out. I don't know when he'll be back. Did you want to see him?'

She did not ask him into the kitchen, where the other two women sat silent.

'I'd like a word with your little boy.'

She was frightened, but that didn't mean anything; she was the kind of woman who would always be frightened, always expecting some disaster.

'He's in bed.'

'I know.'

'He's been up there for over a month.'

'You don't mind if I go up?'

What could she do? She let him pass without daring to protest, as she crumpled a corner of her apron with tense fingers. He had only gone up four or five steps when he saw Marcel coming down towards him, and it was he, Maigret, who stood back against the wall.

'Excuse me . . .' stammered the boy, avoiding Maigret's eye in his turn.

He was in a hurry to get outside, must have expected Maigret to stop him or call him back, but the chief-inspector did neither and continued on his way upstairs.

'The door on the right,' said the mother when he reached the landing.

He knocked. A child's voice said:

'Come in.'

The mother was still standing below, looking up at him while he opened the door and closed it behind him.

'Don't trouble to move.'

Joseph had made as if to get up from the bed where he was sitting with several pillows at his back and one leg in plaster to well above the knee.

'I passed your friend on the stairs.'

'I know.'

'Why didn't he wait for me?'

The room was low-ceilinged, and Maigret's head nearly came up to the central rafter. It was a small room. The bed took up the greater part of it. It was untidy, scattered with illustrated magazines and pieces of wood hacked with a penknife.

'Are you bored?'

There was in fact a chair, but it was heaped with a variety of objects, a jacket, a catapult, two or three books, and some more bits of wood.

'You can take off all that stuff,' said the boy.

Jean-Paul Gastin took after his father and mother. Marcel took after his father.

Joseph resembled neither the butcher nor his wife. He was undoubtedly the handsomest of the three boys, and seemed to be the healthiest and most well-balanced.

Maigret sat down on the windowsill, with his back to the view of yards and gardens, in the place where Marcel had been sitting a few minutes ago, and he seemed to be in no hurry to talk. This was not because he wanted to puzzle the other person present, as sometimes happened at the Quai des Orfèvres, but because he didn't know where to begin.

Joseph opened the conversation by inquiring:

'Where's my father?'

'At Louis's.'

The boy hesitated, then asked:

'How is he?'

Why try to conceal what he must know perfectly well?

'Théo's put him to bed.'

He seemed to be relieved rather than worried by this.

'Mother's downstairs with my grandmother?'

'Yes.'

The sun, now low although the sky was still bright, was gently warming Maigret's back, and the song of birds came up from the gardens; some unseen child was blowing a tin trumpet.

'Wouldn't you like me to take off that plaster?'

It seemed almost as though Joseph was expecting this, he understood the hint. He was not uneasy, like his mother. He didn't seem scared. He was gazing at the heavy figure of his visitor and at his apparently inscrutable face, and considering what line to take.

'You know about that?'

'Yes.'

'Did the doctor tell you?'

'I'd already guessed. What were you up to, you and Marcel, when the motor-bike knocked you down?'

Joseph showed genuine relief.

'You haven't found the horse-shoe?' he asked.

And these words brought a picture into Maigret's mind. He had seen a horse-shoe somewhere. It was while he'd been going round Léonie Birard's house. There had been a rusty horse-shoe lying on the floor, in the corner to the right of the window, not far from the chalk marks which showed where the body had been found.

He had noticed it at the time. He had been on the point of asking about it. Then, as he straightened up, he had caught sight of a nail and reflected that the horse-shoe had probably been hung on that. Many country people will pick up a horse-shoe on the road and keep it, for luck.

Daniélou and his men, who had searched the house before him, must have thought the same.

'Yes, there was a horse-shoe in Léonie Birard's house,' he replied.

'It was me that found it, the evening I had the accident. I was coming along the sea lane with Marcel when I stumbled over it. It was in the dark. I picked it up. We got to the old woman's house and I was carrying the horse-shoe. The window that looks on to the road was open. We crept close up to it without making a noise.'

'Was the postmistress in the front room?'

'In the kitchen. The door was half-open.'

He couldn't prevent himself from grinning.

'First of all I thought of throwing the horse-shoe into the house, to frighten her.'

'Just as you used to throw in dead cats and other filth?'

'I wasn't the only one who did that.'

'You changed your mind?'

'Yes. I thought it would be more fun to put it in her bed. I climbed over the windowsill, without any noise, and went two or three steps inside: then, by bad luck, I knocked into something, I don't know what. She heard. I dropped the horse-shoe and jumped out of the window.'

'Where was Marcel?'

'He was waiting for me, a bit further on. I began to run. I heard the old woman yelling threats out of her window, and that's when the motor-bike ran over me.'

'Why didn't you say so?'

'To begin with, they took me to the doctor, and it hurt a lot. They gave me some medicine to put me to sleep. When I woke up, Father was there, and he began at once to talk to me about the insurance. I understood that if I told the truth, they'd say it had been my own fault and the insurance wouldn't pay up. Father needs money.'

'Did Marcel come to see you?'

'Yes. I made him promise not to say anything either.'

'And since then he's been to see you every day?'

'Nearly every day. We're friends.'

'Isn't Jean-Paul friends with you?'

'He isn't friends with anybody.'

'Why not?'

'I don't know. He doesn't want to be, I suppose. He's like his mother. His mother never talks to the other women in the village.'

'Aren't you bored, staying up in this room all alone for a month?'

'Yes.'

'What do you do all day?'

'Nothing. I read. I carve little boats and people out of bits of wood.'

There were dozens scattered around him, some of them quite skilfully made.

'Don't you ever go to the window?'

'I oughtn't to.'

'For fear people may find out you can walk?'

He answered frankly:

'Yes.'

Then he asked:

'Are you going to tell the insurance people?'

'It's no business of mine.'

There was a silence, during which Maigret turned to look out at the backs of the houses opposite, and the school playground.

'I suppose it's mostly during playtime that you look out of the window?'

'Often.'

Just opposite, on the far side of the little gardens, he could see Léonie Birard's windows.

'Did the postwoman ever notice you?'

'Yes.'

The boy's face clouded at this; he hesitated for a moment, but already knew he would have to tell.

'Even before, whenever she saw me, she used to pull faces.'

'Used she to put out her tongue at you?'

'Yes. After the accident she used to tease me by holding up the horse-shoe.'

'Why?'

'It must have been to make me understand that she might go and tell the whole story.'

'She didn't do so.'

'No.'

The ex-postmistress had behaved rather as though she were the same age as the little boys she used to curse, who made a set against her. She would shout, threaten, put out her tongue at them. She had been reminding Joseph, from a distance, that she could make trouble for him if she chose.

'Did she frighten you?'

'Yes. Father and Mother needed the money.'

'Do they know about the horse-shoe business?'

'Father does.'

'Did you tell him?'

'He guessed I'd done something I hadn't told him about, and he made me own up.'

'Was he cross with you?'

'He said I'd better keep quiet about it.'

'How many times did Léonie Birard show you the horse-shoe through the window?'

'Twenty times, perhaps. She did it every time she saw me.'

Just as he had done in the morning with Jean-Paul, Maigret slowly lit his pipe; his manner was as reassuring as possible. He seemed to be listening absent-mindedly to some trivial story, and his relaxed attitude and innocent face might have led the boy to forget that he was not talking to one of his own school-friends.

'What did Marcel come to tell you just now?'

'That if he was questioned again he'd have to own up.'

'Why? Is he scared?'

'He's been to confession. Besides, I think the funeral made him feel a bit funny.'

'He'll say he saw you at this window before he went across to the opposite window of the schoolroom?'

'How did you know that? You see! Everything goes wrong, in this house. Other people do worse things and nothing happens to them. In our family it's the other way round.'

'What were you doing at the window?'

'I was looking out.'

'The old woman was showing you the horse-shoe?'

'Yes.'

'Tell me exactly what happened.'

'There's nothing else I can do, is there?'

'Not at the point we've reached.'

'I took my rifle.'

'Where was your rifle?'

'In that corner, by the cupboard.'

'Was it loaded?'

An almost imperceptible hesitation.

'Yes.'

'With long or short .22 cartridges?'

'Long ones.'

'Do you generally keep the rifle in your bedroom?'

'Often.'

'Have you ever shot at sparrows through the window, lately?'

He hesitated again, thinking as rapidly as possible, as though he could not afford to make the slightest slip.

'No. I don't think so.'

'You wanted to scare the old woman?'

'I suppose so. I'm not quite sure what I wanted. She was teasing me. I thought she'd end by telling everything to the insurance people, and then Father wouldn't be able to buy a new van.'

'That's what he's decided to do with the money?'

'Yes. He feels sure that if he had a good van and could make a longer round, he'd earn money.'

'Doesn't he earn any as it is?'

'Some months he makes a loss, and it's Grandma who . . .'

'She helps you?'

'When there's no other way. She makes a scene every time.'

'Did you fire the gun?'

He nodded, with a kind of apologetic smile.

'Did you aim it?'

'I was aiming at the window.'

'In other words, you meant to break a pane of glass?'

He nodded again, eagerly.

'Will they send me to prison?'

'Boys of your age aren't sent to prison.'

He seemed disappointed at this.

'Then what will they do?'

'The judge will lecture you.'

'And then?'

'He'll talk severely to your father. The final responsibility is his.'

'Why, when he didn't do anything?'

'Where was he when you fired?'

'I don't know.'

'Was he on his round?'

'I don't suppose so. He never goes off as early as that.'

'Was he in the shop?'

'Perhaps.'

'He didn't hear anything? Nor your mother?'

'No. They didn't say anything to me.'

'Don't they know it was you who fired the shot?'

'I haven't said anything to them about it.'

'Who took the rifle down to the stable?'

This time he blushed, looked around him in

evident embarrassment, avoided meeting Maigret's eyes.

'You can hardly have gone downstairs and across the yard with that plaster on your leg,' insisted the chief-inspector. 'So what?'

'I asked Marcel . . .'

He stopped short.

'No. That's not true,' he admitted. 'It was Father. You'd find out sooner or later, anyway.'

'You asked him to take down the gun?'

'Yes. I didn't explain why.'

'When?'

'On Wednesday morning.'

'He didn't ask you any questions?'

'He only looked at me, kind of worried.'

'Didn't he tell your mother about it?'

'If he had done, she'd have been up here at once to drag the whole story out of me.'

'Does she usually drag stories out of you?'

'She always guesses when I try to tell lies.'

'Was it you who asked Marcel to say he'd seen the schoolmaster coming out of the tool-shed?'

'No. I didn't even know he'd be questioned.'

'Why did he do that?'

'I expect it was because he'd seen me at the window.'

'With the gun. You were holding the gun?'

Joseph was getting hot, but he went on valiantly, doing his best not to contradict himself and not to be seen hesitating.

Although Maigret was still speaking in a colourless voice, without emphasis, as though his words had no importance, the boy was intelligent enough to realize that he was slowly and steadily nearing the truth.

'I don't remember exactly. Perhaps I hadn't picked up the rifle yet.'

'But when he looked through the other window and saw the postwoman fall down, he guessed it was you who'd shot her?'

'He's never said so to me.'

'Haven't you talked it over together?'

'Not until today.'

'And then he simply announced that if he was questioned he'd have to own up?'

'Yes.'

'Was he upset?'

'Yes.'

'And you?'

'I'd like to get it over.'

'But you'd rather go to prison?'

'Perhaps.'

'Why?'

'No special reason. Just to see.'

He refrained from adding that prison would probably be more fun than his home.

Maigret stood up with a sigh.

'Would you have let the schoolmaster be found guilty?'

'I don't think so.'

'You're not sure?'

The answer to this was no. Joseph was not sure. It didn't seem to have occurred to him that he was doing any harm to Gastin. Had it occurred to the rest of the village?

'Are you going away?' he asked in surprise,

as he saw the chief-inspector turn towards the door.

Maigret paused on the threshold.

'What else can I do?'

'You're going to tell everything to the lieutenant?'

'Except about your accident, perhaps.'

'Thank you.'

He did not seem overjoyed at being left.

'You've nothing more to tell me, I suppose?'

He shook his head.

'You're sure you've told me the truth?'

He nodded again, and then, instead of opening the door, Maigret sat down on the edge of the bed.

'Now suppose you tell me *exactly* what you saw in the yard.'

'In what yard?'

The little boy had blushed hotly and his ears were scarlet.

Before replying, Maigret, without having to get up, half-opened the door and said to Marcellin's wife, who was standing at the top of the stairs:

'Please be good enough to go down.'

He waited till she was down below, then shut the door again.

'In this yard.'

'Our yard?'

'Yes.'

'What could I have seen there?'

'That's for you to say, not for me.'

The boy had withdrawn to the far side of his

bed close to the wall and was staring aghast at Maigret.

'What do you mean?'

'You were at the window and the old woman was showing you the horse-shoe.'

'That's what I told you already.'

'Only, the gun wasn't in your room.'

'How do you know?'

'Your father was down there, in the yard, with the stable door open. What was he doing?'

'He was quartering a lamb.'

'From where he was he could see you at your window, and he could see Léonie Birard too.'

'Nobody can have told you all that,' murmured the little boy, more astonished than distressed. 'Did you just guess it?'

'He was quite as much at loggerheads with the old woman as you were. She used to shout at him whenever he went past her house.'

'She used to call him a good-for-nothing and a beggar.'

'Used she to put out her tongue at him?'

'She had a craze for doing it.'

'Then your father went into the stable?'

'Yes.'

'When he came out, he was carrying your gun?'

'What will they do to him?'

'That depends. Have you decided to stop telling me lies?'

'I'll tell you the truth.'

'Could your father still see you then?'

'I don't think so. I'd stepped back.'

'So he shouldn't know you were watching?'

'Perhaps. I don't remember. It happened very quickly.'

'What happened very quickly?'

'He looked around him, and then fired. I heard him growl:

' "There's one for you, you louse!" '

'Did he aim carefully?'

'No. He just lifted the gun to his shoulder and fired.'

'Is he a good shot?'

'He can't hit a sparrow at ten yards.'

'Did he see Léonie Birard fall down?'

'Yes. He stood quite still for a moment, as though he was thunderstruck. Then he rushed into the stable to put away the gun.'

'And after that?'

'He looked up at my window, then went indoors. Later on I heard him go out.'

'Where was he going?'

'To Louis's, to drink.'

'How do you know?'

'Because he came home tight.'

'Was Théo in his garden?'

'He'd just come out of his wine-cellar.'

'Did he see your father fire the shot?'

'He couldn't have, from where he was standing.'

'But he saw you at the window?'

'I think so.'

'He heard the shot?'

'He must have heard it.'

'Your father hasn't said anything to you about it since?'

'No.'

'Nor you to him?'

'I didn't dare.'

'Marcel thought it was you who'd fired?'

'Surely.'

'And that's why he told a lie?'

'We're friends.'

Maigret patted the boy's head with a mechanical gesture.

'That's all, my lad!' he said, standing up.

He was on the verge of adding:

'Some people have to grow up quicker than others.'

What would be the point? Joseph wasn't taking the thing over-tragically. He was so accustomed to little everyday dramas that this one hardly struck him as exceptionally serious.

'Will he go to prison?'

'Not for long. Unless they prove that he was aiming at Léonie Birard and meant to hit her.'

'He only wanted to give her a fright.'

'I know.'

'The whole village will stand up for him.'

After a moment's thought, the boy nodded.

'Yes, I think they will. They're fond of him, in spite of everything. It isn't his fault.'

'What isn't his fault?'

'Everything.'

Maigret was half-way downstairs when the little boy called him back.

'Won't you take the plaster off my leg?'

'It'll be better for me to send the doctor along.'

'Will you send him at once?'

'If he's at home.'

'Don't forget.'

As Maigret reached the bottom of the stairs, he heard a soft:

'Thank you.'

He did not go into the kitchen. The sun was sinking behind the houses, and mist was rising from the ground. The three women were still there, motionless, and watched him in silence as he went past the window.

Outside the church, the *curé* was talking to an elderly woman, and it looked to Maigret as though he felt an impulse to come across the road and speak to him. He, too, must know the truth. He knew about Marcel's lie, from his confession. But he was the only person who had the right to say nothing.

Maigret raised his hat, and the priest seemed rather surprised. Then the chief-inspector went into the *mairie*, where he found Daniélou waiting, smoking a cigar; the lieutenant looked inquiringly at him.

'You can release the schoolmaster,' said Maigret.

'Was it Joseph?'

Maigret shook his head.

'Who?'

'His father, Marcellin.'

'So all I have to do is arrest him?'

'I'd like a word with him first.'

'Hasn't he confessed?'

'He's in no condition to confess anything whatever. If you'll come with me . . .'

The two men walked over to the inn, but as they were about to enter, Maigret remembered a promise he had made, and went along to ring Bresselles's door-bell.

The sister opened the door.

'The doctor isn't here?'

'He's just gone off to deliver a baby.'

'When he gets back, will you ask him to go and take the plaster off Joseph's leg?'

She, too, would be imagining that Joseph was the criminal. The lieutenant was waiting at Louis's door. There was no one standing about outside, now. Ten or a dozen drinkers were still lolling in the taproom, one of them asleep with his head on a table.

'Where did they put Marcellin?' Maigret asked Thérèse.

He had spoken loud enough for Théo to hear. And now it was the chief-inspector's turn to throw the deputy-mayor a sparkling, mischievous glance. Théo, however, proved himself a good loser. Instead of scowling, he merely shrugged, as though saying:

'Well, that's that! It's not my fault . . .'

'The room to the left of the stairs, Monsieur Maigret.'

He went up alone; as he opened the door, the butcher, startled by the sound, sat up and stared at him, wide-eyed.

'Whaddye want, you?' he queried thickly. 'What's time?'

'Five o'clock.'

He swung his feet to the ground, rubbed his

eyes, looked round for something to drink. His breath smelt so strongly of alcohol that the chief-inspector felt slightly sick, and the floor was spattered with vomit.

'The lieutenant's waiting for you downstairs, Marcellin.'

'Me? Why? What have I done?'

'He'll tell you that.'

'Have you been to my house?'

Maigret made no reply.

'You've been pestering the kid?' the butcher persisted, in a toneless voice.

'Get up, Marcellin.'

'I'll do as I please.'

His hair was tousled, his eyes glassy.

'Clever chap, aren't you! Must be proud of yourself! Pestering children! That's what you came here for! . . . And the government pays you to do it!'

'Come down.'

'Don't you touch me.'

He stood up, swaying, and growled:

'All this because the other fellow's a school-master, an educated man, who takes the tax-payers' money too . . .'

He emphasized his contempt by spitting on the floor, staggered out, nearly fell downstairs.

'A *pernod*, Louis!' he ordered, holding tight to the bar.

He wanted to make a handsome exit, was staring round at the others, a forced sneer on his face.

Louis glanced at Maigret as though asking

whether he should serve the requested drink, and the chief-inspector made a gesture of indifference.

Marcellin emptied the glass at one gulp, wiped his mouth, turned to face Théo and declared:

'I got her all the same, the louse!'

'Don't brag about!' the deputy-mayor muttered, looking at the cards in his hand.

'Well, didn't I get her?'

'Not on purpose. You couldn't hit a bullock at thirty yards.'

'Did I get her or did I not?'

'You got her, all right! Now shut up.'

The lieutenant intervened, saying:

'Please come with me quietly, so I don't have to handcuff you.'

'And suppose I want to be handcuffed?'

He was defiant to the last.

'As you like.'

There was a glint of metal, the sound of the handcuffs snapping round the butcher's wrists.

'See that, you chaps?'

He bumped against the doorpost as he went out, and a few seconds afterwards, they heard the slamming of a car door.

Silence fell. The air was saturated with the smell of wine and spirits; thick smoke hovered round the lamp which had just been lit, though it was still daylight outside. In half an hour it would be quite dark and the village would have vanished except for a few spots of light, two or three ill-lit shop windows, an occasional shadowy figure gliding past the house-fronts.

'I'd like my bill, please,' said Maigret, who was the first to speak.

'Are you leaving at once?'

'I'm catching the evening train.'

The others still remained silent, as though in suspense.

'How can I send for a taxi?'

'Just ask Marchandon. He'll take you in his van. He always takes people to the station.'

Théo spoke suddenly:

'Are we playing or are we not? I said spades were trumps. And I'm declaring a *tierce*.'

'With what?'

'The queen.'

'Good.'

'I'm playing the knave.'

Maigret seemed slightly depressed, or tired, as he nearly always did at the end of a case. He had come here to eat oysters, washed down with the local white wine.

'What will you have on me, Inspector?'

He hesitated. The smell of wine-dregs was sickening him. But because of what he had intended before leaving Paris, he said:

'A *chopine* of white wine.'

The light was on in the ironmonger's. One could see past the hanging buckets and pans in the shop to the kitchen at the back, where Marcel Sellier was sitting with a book in front of him, his head between his hands.

'Your health!'

'Yours!'

'You must have a queer opinion of this place?'

He made no reply, and a little later Thérèse brought down his suitcase, which she had packed for him.

'I hope your wife will find everything tidy,' she said.

Actually, it was pleasant to be suddenly reminded of Madame Maigret, of their flat in the Boulevard Richard-Lenoir, and of the brightly lit Grands Boulevards, where he would take her to their usual cinema, the very first evening.

When, sitting in the front of the van, he was driven past the *mairie*, he saw a light in the Gastins' house. In an hour or two the schoolmaster would be home, and the three of them would be together again, as like as three peas, trying to hide away, as it were, on a lost island.

Further on he failed to notice the masts swaying in the darkness to his right, and at the station he bought a whole sheaf of Paris newspapers.

Shadow Rock Farm,
Lakeville (Connecticut),
8 December, 1953.